Murder by Mistake
Rhonda Pohs Mysteries Book Three

Sherry Derr-Wille

Published by Rogue Phoenix Press, LLP
Copyright © 2024

ISBN: 978-1-62420-787-7

Credits
Cover Artist: Designs by Ms G
Editor: Amanda Armstrong

Dedication

I would like to dedicate this book to my many fans who have been requesting murder mysteries for the past several years.

Acknowledgements

As always, I do thank Scott Wasmueller, who is my go to guy for ideas to help out Rhonda as she works on these murders.

Chapter One

"I picked up the costumes for tonight's party," Mark Pohs greeted his wife as soon as she walked through the door after work.

The last thing Rhonda wanted to do was go to a Halloween party, but it was a tradition. Every year they went to the home of one of Mark's co-workers at the high school and spent the Saturday of Halloween weekend with their friends. As usual, she let Mark pick out their costumes.

In the past they'd gone as a saloon girl and cowboy, a pirate and his lady, and a sheik and his harem girl. She wondered what Mark had chosen for their costumes for tonight's party.

"This year we're bound to win the prize for best costume," he declared, waving toward the bag containing the costumes on the couch.

"I'm almost afraid to look in that bag," Rhonda teased. "What will we be wearing this year?"

"Would you be shocked if I told you we were going to be Homer and Marge Simpson?"

Rhonda hoped her horrified reaction didn't show on her face. "Well...if that's what you want..."

"It's not. I was just teasing. We're going as Bonnie and Clyde. Isn't that a kick? When I saw these costumes, I knew my favorite lady cop would make a great Bonnie Parker."

Rhonda giggled as she opened the bag and produced the 1930's style dress, complete with authentic looking guns, hat and a plastic cigar. Mark's costume was complete with a hat, suit, white shirt and tie of the same period.

"This is a hoot," Rhonda said as she held up the dress. "If the guys at work see me in this, it's possible they won't ever let me investigate another murder."

"I doubt that will happen. After the Adkins case this past spring, they're all singing your praises. Changing the subject, what are you taking to add to the buffet table tonight?"

"Don't you ever think of anything other than what you're going to eat?" she teased. "If you must know, I'm making my green bean salad. That always makes a hit at these parties."

~ * ~

Cars lined both sides of the street, indicating the party was in full swing. Because of the crowd already gathered, Mark needed to park a block and a half from the house.

"Did you see old man Richardson sitting on his porch?" Mark asked once they were parked.

"How could I miss him? He's dressed up like a scarecrow with a jack-o-lantern on his head ever since I was a kid. When I was little, you can believe me when I say I never went to his house trick or treating. Of course, once I got older, I found out he was doing it for fun. They also had the best goodies of any house in town."

"You weren't alone. I think every kid in town was scared of that old man at one time or another. Like you say, the older I got, the more I appreciated him. Once I started coaching at the high school, I found out he was a very generous man. When the team needed new uniforms, he was one of the largest contributors."

Before Rhonda could comment, she heard several shots and saw a black SUV speed past her. She caught the first three letters of the license plate but nothing more. Handing Mark the bowl containing her salad and the bag with the accessories for their costumes, she ran in the direction from where the shots seemed to come.

By the time she got to the Richardson house, she heard Mrs. Richardson screaming for help. On the porch, John Richardson sat in his lawn chair, slumped over.

Even dressed as Bonnie Parker, Rhonda carried her cell phone in the garter holding up her old fashioned stockings. "Officer needs assistance. Shots fired!" she ordered into the phone once the operator at the 911 center answered. "This is Detective Pohs. I need backup and an ambulance." She took a deep breath before giving the dispatcher the address of the Richardson home.

Without waiting for help to arrive, Rhonda ran up onto the porch. "You have to help my grandson," Beverly Richardson pleaded.

"Grandson?" Rhonda questioned as she knelt beside the unmoving man in the chair. Not feeling a pulse, she began to panic. Pulling off the fiberglass jack-o-lantern head, Rhonda forced herself not to panic. A bullet had penetrated through the eye cut out and gone into the young man's brain. From the blood staining the shirt, she could tell it wasn't the only injury he'd sustained.

"John's been in the hospital for the last month and our grandson wanted to help me keep the tradition going. He's only seventeen. Will he be all right?"

Two paramedics rushed onto the porch, taking the burden of pronouncing the teenager dead from Rhonda's shoulders.

Phil Mason, Rhonda's partner, seemed to appear out of nowhere. "What happened here, Rhonda?"

Rhonda didn't want to be like the hysterical witnesses she often interviewed, but it took every ounce of strength she possessed to calmly relate the details surrounding the evening. "We were on our way to a party when we heard shots fired. I thought they came from the Richardson house."

"Why this house?"

Rhonda took a deep breath. "For as long as I can remember, John Richardson has dressed up like a scarecrow and sat on his porch during the Halloween weekend. I think every kid in town was scared to death of him at one time or another. As an adult, I've watched for him. It fascinates me that a man of his age would carry on such a tradition."

"The victim didn't look old enough to be doing this for so many years. At least, what's left of his face looks more like a boy than an old man."

"Beverly Richardson told me her husband is in the hospital and her grandson wanted to carry on the tradition. Someone wanted John Richardson dead and killed Sean instead. I've heard Mark talk about the boy several times. He's one of the star players on the football team and because of a silly tradition, he's lost his life." Rhonda could feel her forced control begin to drain from her body as she started to shake.

"I think you should sit down," Phil suggested, helping her to a seat in the squad car. "You're shaking like a leaf."

"I don't know why. I'm a detective. I investigate murders. I don't get emotionally involved."

"Since when?" Phil teased. "It seems to me you and Margie Adkins got very involved during that investigation, to say nothing of the way you and Kitty Reedman bonded when her husband was murdered. Let's go over to that party you were going to tonight. Maybe someone there saw something to help us in this investigation."

"I just thought of something," Rhonda said, putting her hand on Phil's arm to stop him. "When I heard the shots fired, I saw a black SUV peel out like a bat out of hell. I got the first three letters of the license plate. They were JRK."

Phil quickly wrote down the letters Rhonda remembered. "You go on into the party. I'll be there as soon as I call this in to headquarters."

Obediently, Rhonda walked across the street and into the brightly lit house of their friends. As she did, she thought about this neighborhood twenty years ago. Back then, there had only been a couple of houses on the road and it was out in the country. John Richardson owned both farms and rented one of them out. In the early nineties, John's son, Hank, decided he didn't want to run the farm anymore and suggested subdividing both properties. Now it was one of the most comfortable neighborhoods in the county. Unfortunately, Hank Richardson had died of cancer three years earlier and his wife decided it best if she left their country home to move into town to be closer to her job and Sean's school. The only Richardson family living in the area was John and Beverly and from the way it sounded, John may never return home.

"Are you all right, honey?" Mark asked as soon as Rhonda entered the house.

Rhonda nodded.

"What about John?" Trisha Nelson, the hostess for the party, asked. "I was surprised to see him out on the porch. I heard he was in the hospital."

"He is in the hospital. His grandson, Sean, decided to carry on the tradition. I'm afraid it was a fatal decision."

"Oh dear, this will just kill Nancy. First to lose Hank and now Sean, it just isn't right."

Before Rhonda could reply, Phil entered the house. "Can I talk to you, Rhonda?"

Leaving the comfort of not only the house but the companionship of her friends, Rhonda motioned for Phil to follow her out to the back deck so they could have more privacy. "What have you learned?"

"The SUV you saw was stolen from a bar in Clinton last night. It belongs to Ted Jacobs. I don't think he had anything to do with this, but I do want to question him. Do you want to go with me?"

"Well, that's a silly question. Of course I want to be in on this."

"Ah, I think you should think about stopping at your place and changing your clothes. I mean, you look really cute but hardly professional."

"What's wrong..." Rhonda looked down at the forgotten costume. She knew it would look strange for a detective pretending to be the notorious Bonnie Parker to investigate a murder. "I guess you're right. I'll just let Mark know where we're going. Hopefully, you can take me to my place so I can change. That way Mark can have our vehicle to get home."

Mark met her as soon as she came back into the house. "You're going out on this, aren't you?" he asked.

"We've got a lead on that SUV we saw speeding away. Enjoy the party, but I've got to do my job."

"Before you go," Trish said, coming up to where they were engaged in conversation. "Let me take a picture of the two of you for the contest. I'm sure you'll win first prize this year."

Rhonda patiently waited while Trish took at least three pictures of her and Mark posing as Bonnie and Clyde. Earlier in the evening she'd been excited by this party, but the events of the evening told her she had a duty to perform and it didn't include going to a party. The thought of the party going on while across the street the paramedics were preparing

Sean Richardson to be taken to the morgue made her sick to her stomach. It didn't seem right, but in the twenty-first century, people were too self-centered to be overly concerned about their neighbors. It was the nature of the beast.

"I'm sorry, Trish, I have to go. Duty calls."

"I agree with Rhonda," Mark said. "I'll be leaving too." Rhonda headed toward the door when Mark stopped her. "I mean it. I don't want to stay here without you."

"Look, Mark, I'll be working. Besides, I need you here. You can listen to the talk going on at the party or even out in the neighborhood. People will talk to you without even thinking. You're Sean's coach, for God's sake."

"Yes, I am, and I'm taking this hard. I can't imagine staying at this party. I know Trish said she was shocked, but you know how she is, the party must go on."

"And you have to eat. Let's face it, if you go home, you're stuck with green bean salad. I don't have anything else thawed out. Besides, like I said before, I need you to listen to what's going on here."

Mark gave her a kiss and turned to go back into the house. She knew her decision to leave him here was a good one. The topic of the murder would be a hot one at tonight's party.

Phil waited for her next to his car. "Before we head out, I'd like to talk to Beverly Richardson."

Rhonda started to cross the street when Phil stopped her. "This has to be the craziest thing I've ever seen. Who in the hell would shoot at a scarecrow?"

Rhonda turned and looked at her partner. "I can tell you're not from the area. Everyone in town knows John Richardson sits on his porch in that getup for the entire weekend of Halloween."

"Considering the vehicle they used was stolen, do you think it could be gang related?"

Phil's comment took Rhonda completely by surprise. "I'll bet my badge it was planned. If we dig deep enough, we'll find someone who has it in for John."

"That could be, but what you seem to forget is that John wasn't the one to get killed. You were an eyewitness. Can you remember anything else to help us out here?"

"Come on, Phil. You know as well as I do how unreliable eyewitness testimony can be. I told you everything I remembered, especially considering how dark it was."

"In other words, we have zilch in the suspect pool."

Rhonda nodded. "That is, if you don't count every kid John scared over the years. I know the first time I went up on his porch and the scarecrow talked to me, I peed my pants and ran back to where my friend's mother was parked like the hounds of hell were after me. It was the first time I went trick or treating without my mother. She wouldn't let me go this far out of town."

Phil looked around the heavily populated subdivision. "What do you mean so far out of town? I realize this is still tentative in the county, but..."

"But nothing. What you forget is that was thirty years ago. There were only two houses out here, but everyone in school knew the Richardsons had *the best* candy in the area. My friend's mother was only too accommodating to bring us out here. I'm sure she wanted us to be scared out of our wits when John spoke to us."

If the situation hadn't been so serious, Rhonda knew Phil would have laughed at her for being a scaredy cat little girl. She also remembered every adult she ever talked to about John admitted to being just as scared when they were kids. The subject came up every year at the Halloween party.

Chapter Two

Rhonda knew she should have gone home to change clothes, but she also needed to talk to Barbara Richardson. The officers at the scene looked at her skeptically as she crossed the police tape without being able to show her badge.

The remnants of the scarecrow costume, along with the now shattered pumpkin head, littered the front porch of the house, giving Rhonda an eerie feeling. An hour ago, a young man with a bright future wore these bloodstained clothes and in the blink of an eye, his future was gone, and his family changed forever.

Beverly and her daughter-in-law, Nancy, sat in the living room, both apparently in a state of shock. Rhonda wondered how Nancy got out from town so quickly, but decided she probably came out to the farm with her son.

"Who could have done this?" Nancy asked, once Rhonda came into the living room and identified herself.

She was glad she'd left Phil outside to talk with the deputies. Being a woman, she was certain the Richardson women would be more comfortable without a man in the room. "That's what we wanted to ask you. Have either John or Sean received any threats?"

"You have to be kidding," Beverly said. "Ever since John went into the hospital, I've had several people offer to take his place and keep up the tradition. It made him feel so appreciated. I just don't know how we'll ever tell him about Sean."

Rhonda could completely sympathize with the two women sitting on the couch. She'd made several calls on families when there had been a fatal accident while she'd been working on the small town force with Chief Franks. No matter how many times she experienced the shock and hurt of the victims' families, it still bothered her more than she liked to admit.

"Does John have a computer?" she inquired once she regained her composure.

"Yes, why do you ask?"

"It could be he might have received e-mailed threats. If there were, it could help us in our investigation. Can we have one of the deputies take the hard drive down to the office for us?"

Beverly nodded. "I have no idea what you could possibly find. I don't even know how to turn the darned thing on. John keeps saying I should learn how to play solitaire. I don't know how many times I've told him I don't have time for all that nonsense."

Rhonda smiled. She understood how Beverly felt. Although Mark and his father were computer gurus, his mother refused to even touch the keyboard for fear of messing something up.

"What about Sean's computer? Can we take that as well?"

Nancy agreed. "I have his iPod and phone as well. You know how teenagers are these days. They're always texting each other. It used to drive me nuts. Now I wish I could take back every mean thing I said to Sean about his dependence on technology." Nancy burst into tears and Rhonda ached for her.

After a few more questions, Rhonda went back outside to join Phil. "I'm glad you didn't need me in there," he greeted her. "I'm sure this was far more emotional than most of the murder scenes we investigate."

"It was intense. Have there been any further findings out here?"

Phil nodded. "They found shell casings in the street and have sent them down to the lab for analysis. We just received a call saying they also found the SUV."

Rhonda felt a knot form in the pit of her stomach. "Where did they find it?" she questioned, fearing the worst. It was one thing to investigate a murder and another to find the murderers died in a ditch due to a car accident.

"It was crashed on a side road west of Beloit. Of course, there was no one in it when the officers got there. It's being towed into the impound lot so the CSI officers can go over it for fingerprints."

Rhonda sighed deeply. At this point there was nowhere to turn. "Take me back to my place so I can change my clothes. Then we can go over to Clinton to talk to Mr. Jacobs."

It was after nine when Rhonda, looking more like a detective, stood on the porch of Ted Jacobs' home and rang the bell.

The man who answered looked to be about forty or forty-five years old. "Can I help you?" he asked.

"I'm Detective Rhonda Pohs and this is my partner, Phil Mason. We were told you reported your SUV stolen tonight. Is that correct?"

"Yes it is." Rhonda heard the excitement in Ted's voice. "Have you found it?"

"It's been located," Phil began. "Can we come in and ask you what happened tonight?"

"What about my SUV?"

Rhonda could see the terror mirrored in Ted's eyes. "It was totaled. We can get into that later, but for now, we need to get more details."

Ted held the door open and allowed Rhonda and Phil to enter his home.

"What's going on down there, honey?" a woman called from upstairs.

"It's the police about our SUV."

Rhonda glanced toward the stairs and saw a woman about the same age as Ted coming down to join them. It was evident she'd been in the process of getting ready for bed, as she wore a plush pink bathrobe over a nightgown with matching slippers.

"Can you tell us what happened tonight?" Rhonda asked once they were all seated around the kitchen table.

"On Saturday night, Angie and I play darts at the tavern," Ted explained. "Tonight we decided to go a little early and grab a sandwich. We were just finishing our supper when two other couples from our league came in. They were surprised to see us there."

"Why would they be surprised?" Phil inquired.

"Because our car wasn't there," Angie replied. "We laughed about it and told our friends they must be blind since we were parked in the lot behind the tavern. To prove it, Ted went out to the parking lot with them and was shocked to find it gone."

"Was it locked?" Rhonda asked.

Ted nodded. "I know it sounds crazy in a small town like this, but even though our car isn't new, I don't trust anyone anymore. When we got it, we made sure it was tricked out with a CD player as well as a GPS. Stuff like that is gold to these young kids."

"What did you do when you found your vehicle gone?" Rhonda questioned without looking up from her notes.

"We called the village police department and placed a report. Then we had our friends bring us home. We certainly didn't feel much like playing darts."

"Had you been drinking?"

It was evident Ted was becoming frustrated. "I had a beer with our sandwich and Angie had a soda. She doesn't drink, making her our designated driver. What does this have to do with our car being stolen?"

Rhonda finished her notes. "Your vehicle was used in a drive-by shooting in a subdivision outside of Janesville. It was found totaled west of Beloit."

Angie's face went white. "A drive-by shooting? My God, was anyone injured? How could something like that happen?"

"A seventeen year old boy was killed," Phil explained. He went on to relate the story.

"Damn it," Ted gasped. "I know John Richardson. He was a friend of my dad. He even acted as a pallbearer at Dad's funeral. I also knew Hank and his son Sean. This can't be happening."

"Can anyone vouch for your whereabouts tonight?" Phil asked.

"You can't believe we had anything to do with this?" Angie's expression was one of shock.

"It's just procedure," Rhonda assured her. "Do you know how someone got into your vehicle?"

Ted put his head in his hands as though trying to remember every detail of the evening. "The officer said they must have broken out the back side window and popped the locks."

"Do you have a spare key on the vehicle?"

Ted looked up at the question. "I never thought anything about it, but I have a magnetic key box hidden under the lip of the windshield wipers on the underside of the hood."

"If they've done this before, they could start the vehicle without keys," Rhonda said and hoped she'd put Ted's mind at ease. In no way did she believe either of them had any part in the shooting, but they had to get all the facts before passing judgment.

"Are you sure the window was broken out?" Phil asked, making Rhonda wonder how she could have missed that point.

"There was some broken glass where the car was parked. The officer said they were going to send it to the lab for testing."

Rhonda nodded and realized there was little more they could do. For one thing, it was Saturday and for another, it was well after to midnight. It was best to start fresh the next day and get an incident report from the Clinton Police Department.

Chapter Three

Even though it was Sunday morning, Rhonda knew she needed to be in the office early to continue the investigation of the previous night's drive-by shooting. It pleased her when Mark didn't wake up with all her banging around in getting ready for work.

As soon as she got to work, she called the Clinton Police Department and requested a copy of the incident report on the car theft. Moments later, the fax machine rang and she retrieved the report so she could compare it with the report of last night's accident.

"The report from Clinton says there was broken glass at the scene, but not much. Like Ted told us last night, they're planning to send it to the lab for inspection," Phil said.

"I don't think they'll have to. According to the report, the back driver's side window was broken out but not from the accident. None of the other windows was broken, only cracked. There was a lot of damage to the front end and the axle was broken, but the floor of the back seat was full of glass shards.

"I wonder if the hidden key box is still there?"

Rhonda pushed her chair away from her desk. "There's only one way to find out. I know CSI is going over everything, but I doubt they'd even be looking for a spare key."

Phil agreed and grabbed his jacket.

"Well, if it isn't Bonnie and Clyde," Sheriff Cantwell greeted them as they headed toward the door. "I couldn't believe it when one of the deputies told me Bonnie Parker was investigating this murder."

"I certainly didn't plan it," Rhonda said in her defense. "I was on my way to a costume party when we heard the shots."

"And called it in. You also gave a good description of the SUV. Good work, Pohs. Do you have any leads?"

"Not really. We talked to the owner of the vehicle last night. Even though whoever stole it broke out the back window, we want to see if the hidden key is still there."

"Where did the owner say it was hidden?"

Phil described the location and as he did, Rhonda started thinking a bit like a car thief.

"I've got a question," she commented. "If someone shattered the back window, why didn't the alarm go off?"

"You should have read the incident report more closely," Phil replied. "Jacobs may have tricked out the interior of it but, according to the paperwork, it was a nineteen ninety-nine. I doubt it had an alarm system. I'm also starting to think we won't find the key box."

"Why not?" Cantwell questioned.

"Because once they got into the vehicle and popped the hood to hot wire the engine, they'd have to see the key box. If they weren't complete idiots, they would have had to see it. Why go to all the work of hot wiring if they didn't have to?"

"I still want to check it out."

Sheriff Cantwell agreed. "Just don't get in the way of the CSI guys. They get pissed off royally when you interfere with them."

Rhonda soon realized Cantwell knew what he was talking about. The CSI unit was busy dusting the SUV for fingerprints and was none too pleased when Rhonda and Phil wanted to look for the hidden key.

"Could you tell how the thieves got this vehicle started?" Paul asked.

"From what we can tell," the chief investigator said, "They didn't use a key. Instead they jimmied the ignition switch."

Rhonda smiled. "Do you think they would have popped the hood?"

"I doubt it. On something this old, they wouldn't have to. It's surprising though, this thing is loaded with electronic toys and they're still all in place."

"Can we pop the hood, just for the hell of it?" Phil asked.

"You've got to be kidding. The way this sucker is crumpled, there's no way it's going to open."

"Do you mind if I check under the wipers?" Rhonda asked. She knew she could have just done it, but she didn't want to step on the toes of these investigators who were so important to her work.

"I don't know what you expect to find, but go ahead. We won't get anything to link anyone to the murder from that area of the vehicle."

Rhonda smiled as she stood on tiptoe to reach in through the hidden well beneath the wipers. Right away her fingers brushed against the key box. "I'm beginning to agree about the thieves being idiots. They could have saved themselves a lot of trouble if they'd popped the hood." She held up the key box. From the weight of it, she knew it still contained the key.

The CSI tech looked at the key box before going back to dusting the interior for prints. Rhonda knew they wouldn't be able to tell her much about what they found until the information came back from the lab.

~ * ~

Back at their office, Rhonda started making calls to validate Ted Jacobs' alibi for the previous evening. It was almost noon when Rhonda's cell phone rang. The caller ID told her the call came from her husband, Mark.

"What are you and Phil doing for lunch?" he asked as soon as she answered.

"Hadn't given it much thought. Why?"

"We didn't get a chance to talk last night and since you let me sleep in this morning, it didn't happen then either."

"Did you hear anything last night?"

Mark laughed. "I've got a pot of chili on the stove. You've got to eat lunch, so why not save a couple of bucks and kill two birds with one stone? And to answer your question, yes I did hear some things I thought were disturbing."

Phil drove the short distance to Rhonda's house. As soon as they entered the kitchen, the aroma of chili assaulted their nostrils.

"You didn't tell me your husband could cook," Phil commented.

"I don't believe that. I'm always singing Mark's praises. Not only is he a great cook, but he puts up with my crazy schedule, like last night when I ditched him at the party to go to work."

Mark dished up three bowls of steaming chili served with shredded cheese, sour cream, raw onions and French bread. Even though he didn't say anything until they were all seated at the table, Rhonda knew he was anxious to talk to them.

"What did you find out at last night's party?" Rhonda finally asked.

"In the first place, not everyone in that neighborhood is thrilled over John doing his thing every Halloween. They were hoping with him in the hospital the traffic wouldn't be so heavy this year."

"I can't believe they would kill someone over that," Phil commented.

"Maybe they wouldn't," Rhonda added, "but what we don't know is who might have overheard their grumbling."

"Trish told me the neighbors all realize it's a tradition, but they're also concerned about the safety of the kids. Not only does John sit out there on Halloween, he makes a weekend of it. You saw the amount of traffic out last night. I can see where that could get annoying."

"I hear you," Rhonda said, "but the people who live over by the fairgrounds put up with a lot more traffic and more noise for a longer period of time. I can't see putting much blame on the neighbors. They knew about John and his tradition before they built their homes."

"You could be right, but we can't discount it either," Phil replied. "It usually ends up with the guilty party being the last person anyone suspects."

Mark got up to refill their bowls. "Another thing I wanted to talk to you about is tomorrow. Sean was a well-liked kid around school, to say nothing of being a star running back on the football team. I've already talked to the principal about having teams of counselors at the school all day. I was wondering if the two of you could be there as well."

Rhonda thought for a moment. "We'll have to run it past Sheriff Cantwell, but I don't think we could do the whole day. It just depends on what forensics comes up with. We've got them going over the car as well as both John's and Sean's computers."

"Computers," Mark repeated the word as though forming an idea within the confines of his mind. "If you can get one of your technicians into the computer lab at the high school, do you think they'd be able to get in and out today?"

"Today? Why the rush?" Phil asked.

"Because at eight tomorrow morning, you won't be able to get anywhere near them. Computer time is golden for the kids who can't afford personal systems. Besides, if there is anything on one of the computers, you need to find it before any of the kids can destroy it."

"Do you really think someone from the school could be involved in this, honey?"

"I don't want to think so, but not everyone in school is enamored with the jocks. There have been a lot of fights between the jocks, the nerds and the hot kids. I'm not so old that I don't remember my hormones raging in high school. As I recall, someone was always scrapping for a fight. I don't know if anything will come of it, but it could be a lead."

After making a call to the station, Rhonda decided to go to the school with Mark while Phil went back to the office to keep on top of any new information to come in.

"Wow! This set up is really something," Rhonda observed. "When I was in school, our computer lab contained two boat anchors in the library. What are there in this room, twenty five laptops?"

"Make that thirty and they're all chained down. If they weren't, you'd be here investigating a different crime. It would be far too tempting to some of these kids not to make off with them. This room is monitored constantly during the day and for the couple of hours after school lets out. The kids also have to book their time, so if something did come up missing, it wouldn't be hard to find out the name of the last person to use it."

If the number of computers in the high school lab was surprising to Rhonda, the IT department worked the entire area without comment.

"Do you think they'll find anything?" Rhonda asked Mark.

"I don't know if it's what you're looking for, but the district might be interested to know what the kids are doing on their computers.

I've been trying to get them to check out the hard drives of these units for the last two years."

The IT people finally finished just prior to five. With the information from thirty hard drives downloaded to flash drives, they assured Rhonda that by the end of the week, she would have feedback on what they found. This would include the information for John's and Sean's personal computers as well as Sean's other electronic devices.

"What do you say to me taking my best girl out to supper tonight?" Mark asked as they headed toward her vehicle.

"That's the best offer I've had all day. Just let me check in with Phil and I'm all yours." Rhonda placed a call to Phil while Mark got the car started.

"I'm the wrong one to ask," she told Phil. "IT downloaded the information from thirty computers. They assured me we'd have answers by the end of the week. Mark says he's been trying to get the district to do a check like this for a long time. It should be interesting to see what they find. How about you? Did you get any more leads?"

"Not really. I'm sure we can completely clear the Jacobs. They're the innocent victims in this. I just hope they have good insurance.

They talked for several more minutes before calling it a day. After working a full Saturday shift and well into the night investigating the murder, Sunday's full shift had left her exhausted.

"So where are you taking me for supper?" Rhonda asked when she slid into the passenger's seat.

"I know you're tired, but how does Chinese sound?"

Rhonda immediately knew where Mark had in mind. The best Chinese restaurant in town was located above one of the downtown bars, meaning to get there they'd have to climb a steep staircase. "You know my weakness. I always dread those stairs, but I can't turn down steak Kew and egg foo young."

Chapter Four

News of the murder by mistake dominated the news on Sunday, but Rhonda knew most people paid little attention to the weekend newscasts. On the way to work, she listened to the radio long enough to hear how the police were asking the community for any leads in Saturday night's drive-by shooting.

"Were you listening to the news on the way in?" Sheriff Cantwell greeted Rhonda.

"You know I was. Do you have any idea how many calls we'll get today that will lead nowhere?"

"Unfortunately I do, but I don't want you and Phil to be on the phones. I want the two of you to go over to the hospital and interview John Richardson. I checked with his doctor and he says John is strong enough to talk to you. Yesterday I couldn't get permission, but this morning, the doctor told me John asked to talk to you."

Rhonda breathed a sigh of relief. She'd been worried about fielding the crank calls that usually led nowhere fast.

Rather than grab a cup of coffee from the break room, she waited for Phil before heading toward Starbucks. This morning, she knew she needed something stronger than they brewed at the office.

"This must be a high octane day," Phil said, as they drove into the drive-thru lane.

"You bet it is. I need all the fortification I can get to do this interview with John. Hopefully, Beverly will be with him."

At the hospital, Rhonda and Phil bypassed the information desk since they already had the room number. The office had made certain John was moved to another room where a deputy stood guard.

Since they didn't recognize the deputy at the door, both Rhonda and Phil pulled out their badges to gain entry to the room. Once inside, they saw John propped up in the bed with a canella for added oxygen assisting his breathing.

"I'm very sorry for your loss," Rhonda said as she crossed the room to take John's hand in hers for comfort.

"It should have been me," John lamented, gasping for breath after saying just those few words.

"I know the timing is bad, but have you received any threats?" Rhonda questioned.

John shook his head, tears running down his cheeks. "If there had been, I would have never allowed Sean to take my place." The statement had been made in several short bursts as he inhaled deeply after every two to three words.

"You can't possibly believe we would have allowed Sean to take John's place if there were a threat?" Beverly asked, sheer terror in her voice.

"Of course we don't," Phil said quickly. Rhonda knew him well enough to know he was trying to defuse the situation. "These are routine questions. What we're getting at is that the threat could be something thinly veiled or it could have been sent in an e-mail to your computer. If either of you thinks of anything, please feel free to give us a call."

"Thanks," Rhonda said once they were back in the hallway outside John's hospital room. "I'm trained to counsel people at a time like this and not upset them further."

"You didn't do anything wrong, Rhonda. If I'd been lead on this one, I would have asked the same questions. It's procedure."

Before Rhonda could comment, her cell phone rang. "Pohs here," she answered automatically, surprising herself with the professionalism in her voice when her emotions were in such turmoil.

"Hi, honey," Mark greeted her. "Are you and Phil coming over to the high school this morning? The counselors just got here and from what I can see, they've got their hands full. I've been contacted by a couple of members of the football team and they can't believe anything like this could happen to one of their friends."

"We're at the hospital. We just finished talking to John and Beverly. It honestly didn't go well. To be truthful, I opened my mouth and shoved my foot in all the way to the knee. We'll check in with the office and head over to the high school. We should be there in about forty-five minutes."

"Damn, how could I have forgotten about being at the high school?" Rhonda asked once she flipped her phone shut ending the call. "Mark and I talked about it just last night."

"Don't be so hard on yourself," Phil said as they made their way to the car. "I've been at this a lot longer than you. I can attest to the fact the hardest ones you'll ever have to deal with are the ones with kids. Be it murder, accident or illness, it's hard to accept the death of a child."

Rhonda agreed. She knew Halloween would never be the same for her. She recalled her mother saying she never liked May Day because many years earlier a little girl went out delivering May baskets and never returned. Of course, last spring's murder of George Adkins on St Patrick's Day tainted that holiday as well. *How many more holidays will be wrecked with nasty memories while I'm in this profession?*

She immediately chided herself for the negative thoughts. Unlike the May Day disaster over sixty years ago, George's murder had been solved and she was certain this case would come to the same conclusion. She refused to allow it to become one of the cold cases you heard about on television.

~ * ~

The front parking lot at the high school was filled with the usual student-driven cars and trucks as well as vehicles from the local television and radio stations.

A reporter standing in Rhonda's way said, "We're at the high school Sean Richardson attended. Today, in addition to the teachers and students, several counselors have gathered to help the students overcome this tragic loss. I see Detectives Pohs and Mason coming toward me. Can either of you shed some light on this case?" She shoved a handheld microphone in front of them.

"No comment," Rhonda replied, as she walked past the reporter. Even if she had any information, which she didn't, she wouldn't be so unprofessional as to speculate on it outside the department.

Mark met her as soon as she entered the building. Rather than the din of students moving from class to class, the mood was somber.

"I've got someone you should talk to in my office," Mark said.

"Go ahead," Phil advised her. "I'll go down to the cafeteria and see how the counseling sessions are going."

Rhonda nodded and followed Mark to his office. Her mind spun, wondering who she would be meeting and what information he or she could shed on the case.

A young woman sat in the office waiting. She looked too old to be a student, so Rhonda decided she had to be one of the new teachers the districted hired to replace one of the many retirees.

"Rhonda," Mark began, making the proper introductions. "This is Mandy Jennings. She's a new teacher in the English department."

"I'm pleased to meet you, Ms. Jennings. Do you have any information regarding the murder?"

Tears filled Mandy's eyes. "I'm afraid this could be my fault."

"Your fault?" Rhonda questioned, shocked at the young woman's statement. "How could you be at fault in this matter?"

"Washington Irving," she said flatly. "I've always enjoyed *The Legend of Sleepy Hollow*. It only seemed logical to assign it for my senior English class in the fall. I... I never expected it to trigger anything like this."

Rhonda's mind spun back to the reading of *The Legend of Sleepy Hollow*. It was a great read, but in no way would it provoke a drive-by shooting. "Again, why do you think you could be responsible?"

The question seemed to confuse Ms. Jennings. "But it happened over the Halloween weekend and the story is quite frightening. The fact someone shot at a man wearing a pumpkin head on top of a scarecrow costume could be related."

Rhonda nodded, not wanting to totally dismiss Miss Jennings' concept of what prompted the murder. "It's an interesting concept and a hundred years ago I might have even considered it, but with all the violence in the world today through movies and video games, that story is mild by comparison. I'll keep in mind what you've told me, but please don't dwell on it."

Mandy began to cry. "I've never been through something like this. This is my first year teaching, to be truthful, and Sean was one of the most promising students in the senior class. He will be missed."

They talked for several more minutes. For the first time in this case, Rhonda relied on her grief counseling training to put Mandy at ease.

"What do you think about her theory?" Mark asked, once they were alone. "Could life mimic fiction?"

"It could, but millions of people have read the same story since it was written and haven't gone out shooting at jack o' lanterns."

"Agreed. But I guess it's something you have to look at. I mean, these are teenagers we're talking about."

"Teenagers, my dear, who watch violent videos and listen to music our parents would have grounded us for a week if we brought into the house, not to mention the games they play for hours on end. Like I told Mandy, *The Legend of Sleepy Hollow* is very tame in comparison."

Rhonda finished jotting down her notes before going back to the cafeteria with Mark to join the counselors as well as Phil.

Off to one side, she saw a group of football players she recognized. It broke her heart to see the young men who played such a rough game reduced to tears. She wondered if something like this had happened while she was in school if the tough kids in her class would be so deeply moved.

"Who could have done something like this, Mrs. Pohs?" Bernie Frances, the quarterback on the school team, asked.

"We're trying to figure it out. Can you think of anything we can use?"

"I-I can't understand who would want Mr. Richardson dead."

"But Mr. Richardson wasn't there," Rhonda countered. "Didn't you know Sean's grandfather was in the hospital?"

"Ah..."

Someone called Bernie's name and he excused himself, leaving the awkward situation. "That was interesting," Phil said, as Rhonda watched Bernie walk across the cafeteria. "Do you think it's possible Sean would keep something like taking his grandfather's place for the

Halloween weekend a secret? I can tell you, if I was a seventeen year old kid, I'd be excited about carrying on a tradition like that."

"I was thinking the same thing. I've made a note to check on the alibis for all the members of the football team."

One by one, other students came up to Rhonda. Several of the girls confirmed Rhonda's suspicions about Sean's excitement over playing the part of the scarecrow in his grandfather's place. If that was the case, why didn't Bernie, who was supposed to be a close friend, not know about Sean's plans?

Chapter Five

Rhonda sat at her desk reviewing her notes. The hours spent at the school had left her completely drained and no closer to a suspect than she'd been when she first got to work this morning.

Her initial concern about Bernie Frances not knowing of Sean's plans were eased when she checked the attendance records for the last three days of the prior week. Bernie had been absent while attending an out-of-state funeral. In no way could he have talked to Sean.

Other questions crowded Rhonda's mind. Although she knew it would be difficult, she needed to talk to Beverly and Nancy to clarify them. Before leaving the school, she'd placed a call to Sean's mother and now waited for Nancy to arrive.

"I'd like to thank you for coming," Rhonda said as Nancy seated herself across the desk in one of the straight chairs.

"If there is anything I can do to help you find my son's killer, I'll move heaven and earth."

Rhonda breathed a sigh of relief. "First, how are you holding up? Is there anything the department can do to help you?"

"I'm a wreck, but I'll get through this. It's almost as though Sean knew this was coming—or at least, that's what my daughter, Caroline, tells me."

"What do you mean?"

"At the beginning of the school year, Sean told her he'd had a dream. In it, his father told him he was waiting for him in heaven. She said she tried to reason with him by saying he just missed their dad. Caroline told me and I tried to talk to him as well. To my dismay, he continued to be adamant about living his life to the fullest since it wasn't destined to be a long one."

Nancy's revelation hit Rhonda like a ton of bricks. She'd heard about people having premonitions of their own deaths when they were elderly and at the end of their lives, but never from someone so young.

"I know it's hard to believe," Nancy continued. "But I'm half Sioux and my grandfather has always told me I would know when my life was at an end. I've been in contact with him and he says he's been communicating with Sean's spirit and that he's at peace. It's something I have to hang onto."

Rhonda thought about blond haired, blue-eyed Sean and questioned his Native American heritage. Of course, he bore very little resemblance to his mother. To be truthful, he looked exactly like his father, to say nothing of John.

"Do you really believe your grandfather has communicated with Sean's spirit?"

"Very much so. My grandfather is a shaman. I've grown up knowing of his powers. He has also said that, after the funeral he would like to talk to you to see if he can be of assistance."

Rhonda nodded. "I'd appreciate that. At this point, I need all the help I can get. It seems like we've gotten away from the reason I needed to talk to you. Can you tell me when Sean decided to take John's place?"

Nancy wiped the tears from her eyes. "Thursday night, Sean asked me if John was going to be in the hospital for the weekend. I didn't have the heart to tell him his grandfather would probably never come home, so I said he wouldn't be well enough for the Halloween tradition. That was when he decided he wanted to take John's place. At the time, I was so proud of the way he stepped up to the plate. Now I wish I would have told him no."

~ * ~

The next night, Rhonda sat at the funeral home. The family stood in a long receiving line. Nancy stood next to the casket with a younger version of herself who could only be Caroline, standing next to her. The younger woman's hair was very long and although it was not the same dark brown as her mother's, it had several blond and red highlights in it. Rhonda ached for her and made a mental note to interview Caroline after the next day's funeral.

Next to Caroline stood Beverly. She looked so alone, considering John remained in the hospital. Nancy's parents were easy to spot. Her mother was definitely Sioux and her father perhaps of French or English descent. The next in line was a man of perhaps eighty years old along with a very frail woman about the same age. The only thing denoting their heritage was the color of their skin and the fact that the man wore his long gray hair in two long braids trailing over his shoulders and down his back. He wore a three-piece business suit with a perfectly pressed white shirt and fashionable tie. His wife, in contrast, wore her hair in a modern short cut style. Her dress was of the latest fashion, Navy blue with white piping at the sleeves and around the collar. They made an interesting family.

Because of his injuries, Sean's casket was closed and the room was filled with hundreds of pictures of the boy from the day of his birth to the night he took his grandfather's place on the porch wearing the scarecrow costume.

The room was filled with the same students she'd seen at the high school during the counseling session. Each one passed by the closed casket. The boys tried to put on a brave face, while the girls cried inconsolably. Along with the students, floral arrangements filled every unoccupied area of the room, including around the spaces and between the easels holding the pictures.

Rhonda had been the first person to go through the receiving line to pay her respects, so she could sit back and watch the mourners waiting to do the same. It didn't take long for the front of the area near the casket to be filled with everything from single flowers to footballs, all left by Sean's friends.

With the exception of the elderly shaman, all the adults in line alternated between tears for their loss and laughter at stories related by Sean's friends.

"My granddaughter told me you are the detective trying to find my great-grandson's killer. She would not have had to tell me this, as I saw you in my dreams."

Rhonda jumped at the sound of the old man's voice. She certainly hadn't seen him leave the reception line. She only remembered him standing there talking to the young mourners, but somehow he now sat at her side. *Was it possible he had supernatural powers?* "In your dream?" she echoed his words in the form of a question.

"When my granddaughter called to tell me of Sean's murder, I already knew. As soon as Sean's spirit left his body, he came to me in a vision to tell me he'd been reunited with his father and the ancestors. At the same time, I saw you looking for his murderer."

Rhonda looked skeptically at the old man. "Your vision didn't tell you who it is I'm looking for, did it? It would certainly make my job easier."

"I wish it had. Sean's killing was not a face-to-face thing. Had it been, perhaps I could have given you a description. I can tell you the spirits will guide you. I have told my granddaughter I want to be of assistance to you. Although my wife is not well and will be returning to our home, I vowed I would not join her until those responsible for Sean's death are in your custody."

The old man touched Rhonda's hand and returned to the reception line as though he had never sat at her side.

"How much do you know about Native American shamans?" she asked when Phil finally joined her at the funeral home.

"Enough to be afraid of them. These old boys have powers no one in this day and age can understand. When I was a kid, my folks were into going to pow-wows. At one of them I went to, there was a ceremony conducted by a group of those old men. They scared the shit out of me."

"Nancy's grandfather is a shaman. He told me he wants to help us. I just don't know how much of this I believe."

Phil glanced over at the old man. "I say we take any help he can give us. He looks harmless now, but if you could see him in full regalia, I think you'd understand his power."

~ * ~

The next morning, the line of cars from the church to the cemetery stretched for over two miles. Even though the weather was relatively warm for the first of November, the forecast was for snow.

The hearse arrived at the cemetery and the members of the football team acted as pall bearers and honor guards. Rather than the minister saying the words of comfort, Nancy's grandfather, in full regalia, chanted and prayed to the Great Spirit in his native tongue.

If Rhonda ever doubted what Phil had said about the impact of seeing the old man in his element, seeing for herself made her a believer. She found the ceremony chilling. *Could this old man see into the future? If he could, would he be able to help them solve this case?* She had her doubts, but as her grandmother used to say 'any port in a storm.'

The young people seemed to be fascinated by what Rhonda could only describe as a macabre performance. For some reason, she knew she'd be delving more deeply into the traditions of the Sioux than she ever intended.

"Sean was studying with my grandfather during the summer," Nancy said as she sat next to Rhonda at the luncheon put on by the ladies of the church. "Even though he was Christian, Sean wanted to learn the ancient ways of our people as well. Grandfather said he was a good student, but he would never be a shaman. It is a good thing he has other grandsons and great-grandsons to follow in his footsteps."

"He offered to help us. I'd like to take him up on his offer, but I don't even know his name or how to contact him."

"My grandparents are staying with me. Grandfather's name is Richard Brave Beaver and my grandmother is Loretta. I'm so glad they're staying with me. I don't know if I'm ready to stay in the house alone. Of course, I'm not thrilled to have my grandmother return home alone, but she needs to go back to her own doctor for her treatments."

"What about your parents and your daughter?"

"Mom and Dad will be going back to Minneapolis in the morning. They both have classes to teach. They also have to try to explain this to their Lakota students."

"Lakota?"

"There are a lot of Sioux who have gone to Minneapolis in search of better jobs. They want their children educated in the Native American school there. Dad is the principal and Mom has been teaching math ever since she graduated from college. It's a great school. I graduated from there and thoroughly enjoyed it, especially the Native American studies they offer. As for my daughter, she's in her junior year at UW Eau Claire. We all feel a college education is very important. Sean wouldn't want her sitting around here mourning while she could be studying."

"So what will you do when your grandparents have to return home?"

"I don't know. This is home, but without Hank and Sean, it will be empty. It's going to take a lot of consideration."

Rhonda agreed. She certainly couldn't imagine being without Mark for the rest of her life.

Chapter Six

The morning after the funeral, Richard Brave Beaver arrived at Rhonda's office unannounced. For some reason, Rhonda wasn't surprised. The man seemed to have the ability to appear and disappear at will. It made her wonder if he indeed had supernatural powers.

"Do you have time to speak with me?" he asked before entering Rhonda's cubicle.

"Of course I do."

"Can we talk here or do we need to go into your interrogation room? You see, I do watch cop shows on TV."

Rhonda laughed. Somehow, she couldn't imagine this man watching *Law & Order* the way Mark did.

"My office is a bit cramped and I would like my partner and Sheriff Cantwell in on our discussion. I don't think we need to go to the interrogation room, but we do have a comfortable conference room." In her mind, she wondered how at ease Mr. Brave Beaver would be in the plush captain's chairs or if sitting on the ground in front of a campfire would be more to his liking.

"It sounds agreeable to me," Richard replied.

Rhonda picked up the phone on her desk and called Phil as well as Sheriff Cantwell to join them. "Do you mind if we tape record our session?" she asked as they made their way to the conference room.

"I would expect it. Even though I am not a suspect, I know such things are best recorded so there is no question as to what has been said."

Once they were all seated in the conference room and the proper introductions were made, Richard began to speak.

"Before my grandson-in-law went to join the ancestors, I saw very little of my great-grandson. At his father's funeral, it was Sean who sought me out. He had many questions about the way of life of our people. My granddaughter agreed it was something he should know, so he spent last summer with my wife and me. He wanted to become a shaman and begin his studies."

Rhonda made notes furiously, even though she knew every word the old man spoke was being recorded. Sometimes her notes were more helpful, since it allowed her to refer back to them and see the asked questions and answers she knew she would forget later.

"Even though Sean was older than most of the young men who go on their vision quests, he wanted to join them in this age old ritual of passage. He came back a changed young man. He expected to learn of his Spirit Guide. Instead, he saw his future. He told me his life would be a short one and would end violently. I was afraid the realization would send him back to his mother in fear. Instead he became a man. He looked forward to being reunited with his father, as well as the ancestors. He said if his life was not to be long on this earth, he looked forward to walking with the ancestors and learning of the history of our people. He also said he didn't want anyone to mourn him, for he would be where there would always be peace."

Tears formed in Rhonda's eyes. Could she so easily accept such a premonition? She doubted it. "Do you have any other information for us?" she finally asked.

"I have conferred with the ancestors, but those who have done this terrible thing have hidden their faces from them. When you find those responsible, you will learn this was well planned."

They talked for several more minutes. The old man's conviction that he was actually connected to the spirit world amazed Rhonda. Although he was sincere, she knew they could put very little stock in the information he gave them.

~ * ~

Several hours later, Rhonda sat in her office going over the reports from the IT department on what they'd found on Sean's electronic gadgets, as well as the computers from the school and the one they'd confiscated from John's home.

The information from the high school computer lab was enough to make Rhonda sick to her stomach. It soon became apparent that either the school put no protective locks on the computers so certain sites couldn't be accessed or the kids knew how to bypass them. Porn sites had been accessed whether out of curiosity or because of pure interest, Rhonda didn't know.

"I just finished going through Sean's cell phone," Phil said as he entered Rhonda's cubicle. "There are some interesting text messages. Now all we have to do is figure out who belongs to which screen names. So far we've found out Sean is Medicine Man. Other than that, we found a message from a Mad Max on Saturday morning."

Rhonda perked up. "What did it say?" she asked excitedly.

"As far as I can figure out, it says, 'have fun tonight, scarecrow boy.'"

Rhonda checked the register for the names of classmates as well as members of the football team. "It could be either Evan Maxwell or Max Cleary. They're both in the senior class and on the football team. I think we should talk to both of these young men."

Phil agreed and together they went to the high school to inquire about the class schedules for both of the boys. They found Evan Maxwell in study hall and Max Cleary in the gym for physical education.

While Phil questioned Evan, Rhonda took Max into Mark's office. "Am I under arrest for something, Mrs. Pohs?" Max asked, his hands trembling.

"Relax, Max. We've just found some text messages on Sean's phone and we're checking on screen names. What is your handle? We know Sean was Medicine Man."

"I-I'm Mad Max," the boy stammered. "Are you talking about the text where I called him scarecrow boy?"

"Yes, I am. What did you mean by it?"

Max took a deep breath. "Sean and I were pretty tight. He was so into the business of becoming a shaman, I was surprised when he said he was planning to take his grandpa's place last weekend."

"Why was it a surprise?" Rhonda asked. "I've been told Sean and his grandpa were very close."

33

"You hit the nail on the head," Max agreed. "They were close before he went to South Dakota last summer to stay with his great grandparents. His mom is into all that Native American stuff, but I didn't think his dad was thrilled about it. After his dad died, all Sean could talk about was going to the reservation. I thought he would come back seeing how backward it all seemed. Instead, he came back and said he wanted to be a shaman."

"Why was that such a shock?"

"Up until last spring, Sean and I were looking into going to UW at Madison on football scholarships. After he came back from the reservation, he only wanted to go back and study with his great-grandpa. He still played one hell of a football game, but he was doing it for fun and not in the hopes of getting a scholarship."

"Then your message didn't mean anything derogatory?"

"Derogatory? You mean like a threat? No way. It was more of a joke. I gave him a hell of a lot of credit for wanting to carry on the tradition, even if I did think it was sort of silly. Now I wish I'd tried to talk him out of it."

Tears flowed from the teenager's eyes. It almost broke Rhonda's heart. Losing a friend to a traffic accident or a long illness was much more acceptable to a young man than losing one to a random murder. She knew Max would never get over Sean's death. She also hoped he would learn just how precious every life was and how quickly it could be snuffed out.

"Life is too short to worry about 'what if' and 'I wish I would have.' What I need from you is to keep your ears open. If you hear anyone bragging or see anything out of the ordinary, you know how to get in touch with me. Oh, one other thing, can you help us out another way?"

"Anything. What can I do?"

"We have Sean's cell phone. Do you think you can stop down to my office and see if you can decode the screen names? You kids seem to talk in a language us old folks don't understand."

"You bet, and Mrs. Pohs, I don't think you're old."

Rhonda smiled. A compliment, even one coming from a teenager trying to be polite, was something to be pleased about.

"I struck out with the Maxwell boy," Phil said when he entered Mark's office. "How did you do with Cleary?"

"He's Mad Max, but the text was sent out of respect and not as a threat."

"How can you be so certain?"

"Because Max and Sean were best friends. He was confused by Sean's change after he came back from South Dakota, but he respected his friend's choice."

"So where do we go from here?"

Rhonda smiled. "Max said he'd come down to the office after school and help us with the screen names."

~ * ~

Grateful for any help she could get, Rhonda went back to the office to go over more of her notes before Max came. Even though Phil had been skeptical, she knew the boy would arrive just as he promised.

By four-thirty, Rhonda was beginning to doubt her faith in the teenager she'd met earlier in the day. She was just getting ready to leave for the day when she heard someone enter her office.

"I'm sorry I'm late, Mrs. Pohs," Max said. "I didn't know if I should really come down here, so I went to football practice and talked to Coach. He said I owed it to Sean. I guess he's right. I want to help any way I can." Rhonda smiled, pleased her misgivings had been in vain. "I don't want to keep you too late. I know you must have a ton of homework. I have a list of screen names from Sean's instant messages and text messages. I'd appreciate it if you could take them home tonight and work on decoding them. If you get them done tonight, I'll be happy to come over to your house and pick them up. That way I can talk to your folks at the same time. They should know what a good kid they have."

Chapter Seven

"What can you tell me about the time Sean spent with you last summer?" Nancy asked.

Richard shook his head in despair. Before answering his granddaughter, he took a drink of the coffee sitting in front of him. The last thing he wanted to do was to tell his granddaughter about the visions both he and Sean experienced last summer. He'd been a shaman for too many years not to take heed of what the spirits told him.

"I don't know if you are ready to know such things. It was a time of learning and growth for Sean."

From the look on Nancy's face, he could see her exasperation with him for withholding information about her son. How could he tell her the Great Spirit as well as the Spirit Guide had not been positive about Sean's future?

"I knew something spiritual happened to him while he was with you last summer. He was changed when he came home, but he wouldn't talk about it to me. It might have been different if his father were still alive. He really needs a man to talk to. There are so many things boys don't want to talk to their mothers about."

"You are right about Sean needing male companions. He bonded with many of the men and boys on the reservation."

Visions, or perhaps they were memories, crowded his mind. In them he could see Sean sitting among the men as the drums beat out the age-old rhythms and the singers put voice to the stories he'd heard since childhood and never tired of reliving. It was amazing to watch as his great-grandson heard them for the first time and finally understood their meaning.

Once again he sat in the main room of his home. It was not a lodge made from the hide of the buffalo, like the one where he'd grown up. Instead, he now lived in a modern home purchased by the reservation. His wife often longed for the old way of life, but admitted she much preferred her manufactured home, as it was much easier to keep clean, to say nothing of her modern kitchen.

"Grandfather," Sean had said after watching the dancing at the sacred circle. "Would I be able to live here if I wanted?"

The question caught Richard completely off guard. "This is not an easy life and it is not the one into which you were born. The decision is one to which you should give much thought and prayer. In Wisconsin you could go to college and take over the assets of your father's business. If you want to return here, I would insist you go to college as well. An education will do much for our people."

"But I want to be a shaman like you. How can I learn that in college?"

"You can learn many things. If you are meant to be a shaman, it is something I can teach you when the timing is right."

"I know you were born to this life as was my grandmother, but why is it you don't move to the city like Grandma and Grandpa?"

Richard gave his answer much thought. "My daughter was born and raised here, but I wanted special things for her, just as I do for you. That was why I insisted she go away to school. There she met your grandfather. I was disappointed when he was white, but he has become like a son to me. His life's work is teaching in the school for Native American children in Minneapolis, just as my life's work is here among the people. There are so many roads for you to travel, consider each of your options carefully."

Sean sat for a moment. "You know I went on a vision quest."

Richard nodded. He knew the vision quest had been something his great-grandson wanted to do, but he'd been skeptical. Since Sean was only one quarter Sioux, Richard had no idea if the spirits would be receptive to the boy.

"Did the spirits speak to you?"

"Grandfather," Nancy said, her voice sounding with concern. Her one word shattered the memory of the past summer. "Are you all right?"

"Yes, Granddaughter, I am all right. I was remembering Sean's summer visit to the reservation."

Nancy's eyes filled with tears. "Sean told me he went on a vision quest, but he wouldn't say much about it. He said what happened was between him and his Spirit Guide. Did he tell you about it?"

"He told me he has a Spirit Guide, but it wasn't until he joined the ancestors that the things that he experienced have been made known to me. What he did tell me was the Spirit Guide told him he would walk with the ancestors soon and he would meet a violent death."

Nancy sobbed as though her heart would break. "Was-was he frightened?"

"I honestly don't think so. His Spirit Guide was the wolf and it made him very strong. He has communicated with me from beyond the grave and told me his soul has rejoiced at being reunited not only with his father but also with his Sioux ancestors. They have welcomed him."

"But why, Grandfather? Why would the spirits want someone so young to join them?"

"You must trust me when I say his purpose in this life has been fulfilled. You have no idea how many lives have been touched by your son."

"Oh, Grandfather, who would want to kill him?"

"That is one thing the ancestors have not told me. I do not know if the bullet fired on Saturday night was meant for John or Sean. It is not something I am meant to know. As I said earlier, Sean's Spirit Guide predicted his early death."

Richard wished his words could have given his granddaughter comfort. Among his people he was known for the way he could not only heal physical wounds but also the ones that plagued the mind.

I am sorry my mother is so sad, Sean's voice sounded in Richard's mind. *You must take her back to the people.*

She must see this was meant to happen.

Who did this to you Sean?

You know I cannot tell you that which is unknown to me.

Although the voice belonged to Sean, Richard knew the words came from the Great Sprit to give him comfort. The Great Spirit knew all, but for some reason the motive behind Sean's killing, as well as the name of the killer, was being withheld from him.

Richard returned his attention to Nancy. "What will you do now, Granddaughter?"

Nancy looked up at him. "I don't know. I honestly don't know. John and Beverly need me and I have friends here, but there are also some terrible memories. I'm not sure I can continue on without Sean and Hank."

"Then come home with your grandmother and me. Let the people help you heal and come to grips with the future you are now forced to face alone. I know you feel obligated to John and Beverly as well as to your daughter, but this is a time for you to take care of yourself. As you know, the days of our lives are sometimes very short. You need to connect with your people and find your Spirit Guide. It is never too late."

He watched as Nancy contemplated his suggestion. Although she had lived her entire life in the white world, he knew the pull of her heritage would bring her back to the life she should have lived and give her new direction.

Chapter Eight

"I think I might have found something," Kyle Hoeffstater from the IT department said when he entered Rhonda's cubicle.

Rhonda looked up. This case had her completely baffled. They'd been over everything with a fine tooth comb and still had no more leads than they had on Saturday night.

"Something?" she questioned.

"Yes, ma'am."

She hated it when younger guys called her ma'am, but she knew someone as young as Kyle must think she was ancient.

"I finally got through the five hundred e-mails in John's spam folder. This one didn't look suspicious, but that's why I took the time to read through them all."

Kyle handed Rhonda a printout of the e-mail he was talking about. The words on the paper practically jumped out at Rhonda.

Hi Pumpkin Head—Halloween is coming—Are you ready? Can't wait to see you again.

Of course, the message wasn't signed. Stuff like this never was. "Do you have any idea who sent this?" she finally managed to ask.

"We're working on it. This guy used an obscure site, one that's almost impossible to track, but we're working on it. It's the first lead we've had since the text messages on the kid's phone, so we have to work harder to find out who this is. I should have something for you by the first of next week."

Rhonda sighed. She wished this investigation would go faster, but the leads were few and far between. She was grasping at straws, but it seemed as though that was all she was going to get.

Kyle left the office and Rhonda again scanned the printout in front of her. When her phone rang, she answered it, almost absently.

"Pohs here."

"Rhonda, this is Nancy. I've been out of the house a lot lately, so I just got your message. Have you had any leads?"

"I'm sorry to say we haven't. What I need to know is if Sean had any girlfriends we should know about."

There was a brief silence on the line. "Let's see, before Sean went to South Dakota last summer, he was dating Crystal Davis. They split on good terms. She wanted to date other people over the summer and he agreed. I thought they'd get back together when he came back home, but she was dating Mike Yankston. He took Jennifer Riley to the homecoming dance a couple of weeks before..."

The pause brought a lump to Rhonda's throat. *How long would it take for Nancy to admit her son had been murdered?*

"They weren't serious. It was just a date. Since he was going to be the homecoming king and wasn't dating anyone, he thought the student body should choose the queen. It went against everything any of us ever heard of, but it worked out well. Jennifer is a rather quiet girl. You know the kind, a bookworm and not one of the 'in' girls. Everyone was shocked when she was voted queen. Otherwise, he's been with the guys or just hanging out at the house. I was pleased about it, because I thought he was too young to get involved with a girl. The last thing I wanted was for him to announce he'd gotten someone pregnant. I guess I don't have to worry about that anymore, do I?"

Nancy's unanswered question hung between them with silent urgency. Rhonda had no answers for the woman who had suffered two horrific losses in a little over a year.

"Are you still here?" Nancy asked.

"Oh yes, I was thinking about what you said. I know it's not much comfort at this point, but one day you will be a grandmother."

"I know I will, but right now the hurt of losing both Hank and Sean so close to one another is more than I can stand. My grandfather has suggested I go back to South Dakota with him and my grandmother. It's not like wintering in Florida or Arizona, but it's what I need."

"What about John and Beverly?"

"We've talked about this. They agree with my grandfather about this trip. It's not like they'll be here alone. They do have two other sons and two daughters in the area. If anything happens to John, I won't be that far away from the airport. I can be back in Madison in a matter of hours."

"Then I do wish you luck. Please make certain I'm able to contact you. Of course, if you can think of anything else, you have my cell number."

"I know and I promise to keep in touch."

~ * ~

Nancy hung up the phone. When her grandparents first suggested she go back to South Dakota with them, she'd been appalled by it, but everyone from her friends to Beverly and John insisted it was the right thing to do.

Only her parents seemed to be against it. They gave her the same arguments they'd made last summer when Sean wanted to spend time on the reservation. They said they'd broken with the old ways and there was no use in dredging up the past, especially when it was a dead one. They were Christian and although they loved her grandparents dearly, they couldn't accept a religion that wasn't based around the church.

Nancy hadn't listened to their arguments last summer and she certainly didn't want to listen to them now. She knew her grandfather not only practiced the old ways but he also loved the Lord. It was his contention the Great Spirit and God were one in the same. The only difference was living so closely with nature, he was more easily able to communicate with his higher power.

As much as Nancy wanted to drive out to South Dakota, she finally agreed to fly back home with her grandparents.

Before leaving, she went out to the cemetery. A light snow had started to fall as she reached the area where Hank and Sean were resting side by side. The scarred earth of Sean's grave stood in direct contrast to the sod-covered side of Hank's gravesite. With the way the snow was falling, both graves would soon look identical.

"I came to tell you I'm going to South Dakota to stay with

Grandpa and Grandma for a while. I can't stay here alone."

You know it's for the best, Hank's voice reassured her. *Sean has told me you need to be with your people. Our son has explained the power of the spirits on the reservation to me.*

Nancy wiped away the tears coming to this place always prompted. In the morning she would be flying from Madison to South Dakota. This afternoon she needed to go to the hospital to say goodbye to Beverly and John. Although Beverly's health was good, it was doubtful she would ever see John alive again.

"You're doing the right thing, Nancy," John said. "I've had some long talks with your grandfather while he's been here for the funeral. He's a wise man. Allow him to help you heal. I respect you staying here after Hank's death. I know you did it so Sean could continue to go to school with his friends. Now it's time for you to take care of yourself."

Nancy thanked her in-laws and left the hospital. Later in the afternoon, her grandparents helped her pack up her belongings and prepare the house to be rented. She'd been lucky when her neighbor's son approached her about renting it for him and his new wife while they built their home. Since the work couldn't begin until spring, she would have a full year to come to grips with her loss and make a decision about her future.

~ * ~

Rhonda stared at the phone long after the connection was broken. She wondered if she would be able to pack up everything and move to another state to close the door on such a painful past.

The pad on the desk contained the names of two more people they would need to interview. Crystal Davis possibly felt betrayed when Sean went to South Dakota for the summer. Nancy made Jennifer Riley sound more like a social date and nothing else.

Again she checked the class roster to get information on the two girls. Jennifer lived in a new subdivision east of town, while Crystal's parents had a home relatively close to the one Nancy would soon be leaving behind.

Rhonda placed a call to Vern Davis to set up an appointment to talk to Crystal.

"I don't see why you want to talk to my girl," Vern groused. "She don't know nothing about who killed that half-breed."

"I want to talk to her because she used to date Sean."

"Well, she's dating Mike now. Sean is ancient history. Why aren't you talking to that little bimbo, Jennifer? Sean took her to the homecoming dance. I think it damn near broke my little girl's heart. You only have to look at the two of them side by side to see my Crystal is a hundred times more beautiful than Jennifer. Of course, you can't even try to think what those Indian boys think about white girls."

Rhonda shook her head. She was glad Vern couldn't see her doing it. How in the world could anyone even think of Sean as a half-breed when he had such beautiful blue eyes and blond hair? If he hadn't told people of his heritage on his mother's side of the family, no one would have even guessed at it.

"I think that's all the more reason I need to talk to both girls. Since they're seventeen, I need to have a parent with them. It's for their protection as well as mine."

"From what I hear, you didn't have parents at the high school when you talked to Evan and Max. What kind of bullshit were you pulling?"

"You know better than to think I'd do anything underhanded. Evan and Max are both eighteen. I'm trying to solve a murder. When I get a lead, I intend to follow it up."

After her confrontation with Vern, Rhonda finally set an appointment for Saturday morning at nine. Building up her courage, she placed a call to the Riley home.

"Why do you want to talk to Jen?" Mary Riley asked.

"I'm talking to everyone who was close to Sean. Nancy told me Sean took Jennifer to homecoming. I was wondering if you or your husband could come in with Jennifer on Saturday at ten?"

"Of course we can. We'll do anything we can to help find Sean's killer."

"Well, that went better," Rhonda said aloud to no one in

particular.

"Better than what?" Phil asked, as he entered her cubicle carrying two cups of coffee.

Rhonda took her cup and tasted what she knew would be a very bitter brew. "I just talked to Nancy and she told me about the girls Sean dated before his murder. I'm meeting with Crystal Davis and her dad at nine on Saturday morning. Jennifer Riley and her parents are coming in at ten. The Riley's were okay with it, but I think Vern is coming in with the idea of chewing my head off. It should be interesting, to say the very least."

Chapter Nine

Saturday morning, Rhonda braced herself for the meeting with Vern and Crystal Davis. As much as she would have wanted Crystal's mother, Sheila, to come with them, she wasn't surprised to see Vern come in without her. Rhonda knew Vern well enough to understand his position when it came to women. Even though Sheila worked as the manager of a small insurance office, she knew her place when it came to her marriage. Vern was the boss and that was that.

They were already sitting in the conference room when Rhonda and Phil came in to start the interview.

"You sure took your good-natured time in getting here," Vern snapped. "We've been waiting..."

"Look, Vern," Phil said, taking the defensive position. "Your appointment is for nine and it's now eight fifty-five. We planned to get here early to have everything set up. It looks like you beat us to the punch."

"Isn't it your job to be here when the people you're interrogating arrive?" Vern retorted.

"To begin with, Vern, it doesn't matter who came first," Rhonda replied as calmly as possible, "This isn't an interrogation. We just want to talk about Crystal's connection to Sean."

Rhonda remembered seeing Crystal at the visitation. Like most of the teenage girls, she'd cried bitterly, draped herself over the closed casket and left with mascara running down her cheeks. Today, like that night, her make-up was applied perfectly, including dark eyeliner as well as black mascara thickly coating her lashes.

Before speaking, Crystal took one of the tissues from the box on the table and dabbed at her still dry eyes. "Sean and I went steady last spring," Crystal finally began. "Then he went out to South Dakota and, well, I got lonely. That's when I started dating Mike. He said he was certain Sean was getting his share of Indian tail and he would want me to have a good summer."

The look on Vern's face told Rhonda Crystal's sexual activity came as no surprise. It was possible the girl was on the pill and Sean had not been her first 'steady' boyfriend.

"Mike said he should have been homecoming king, since he was a senior just like Sean."

Rhonda's mind spun. It didn't matter if there were other seniors on the team, the one who held the position of captain usually became the homecoming king. If Mike had been king, that would have made Crystal queen, and Rhonda had no misconceptions about what Crystal wanted for herself. She certainly didn't want to be one of the girls on the court. Her ambition was to have the spotlight. If she and Sean had continued dating, there would have been no doubt she would have worn the crown on the night of the dance.

"Were you and Mike on the homecoming court?" Rhonda finally asked.

"Of course we were. All the seniors on the team and their dates were on the court. It just wasn't fair that Sean wasn't dating anyone. Who would have ever thought he would have insisted on the school voting on someone to be his date?"

"Were you in the running to be queen?"

"No way. The girls they were voting on were all the losers who weren't dating anyone. I was dating Mike and everyone knew I would be on the court, so I couldn't run for queen. Even if I had been able to run for queen, Mike wouldn't have allowed it. He said there was no way he wanted me to be with Sean for all the activities when I should be with him."

Rhonda almost felt sorry for Crystal. She doubted Sean had treated Crystal in such a controlling way. It was entirely possible she was looking for someone exactly like her father and had found another controlling man to be in her life.

"Is Jennifer one of your friends?" Phil asked.

Crystal looked as if someone had just slapped her in the face. "I'd never be friends with anyone like her. She's not one of the popular girls. She doesn't even use make-up or go out with any of the cool guys at school. What's even worse is she's on the honor roll, not the cheerleading squad."

Rhonda watched Crystal. The girl seemed to be confessing her true feelings about Jennifer, but could she be believed?

"Did you know about Sean taking his grandfather's place for Halloween?"

Crystal chewed her lower lip. "He might have said something about it. I didn't pay much attention. I'm with Mike now and what Sean does on his own time is of no concern to me. Mike says what a half-breed does is of no consequence to us."

Rhonda noticed the look of skepticism on Phil's face. *Was it possible this teenage girl could be capable of plotting a murder?* If she were, it certainly would not have been Sean on the receiving end of her rage. From the body language she displayed, Crystal was still in love with Sean. Her anger was aimed more at Jennifer, who had taken her place as homecoming queen.

"I think you've harassed my daughter enough," Vern declared. "We're finished here."

"We don't consider investigating a murder harassment," Phil said, defusing the situation. "For now, we have all the information we need. We'd like to thank you for coming in today."

Rhonda watched as Crystal got to her feet and flipped her long hair as though preening for some unseen camera. *Someday this spoiled little girl will wake up in the real world, without Daddy to intervene for her.*

"I hope the cops ream out your skanky ass," Rhonda heard Crystal say.

Looking up she saw Jennifer and her parents waiting to be interviewed. The confrontation gave Rhonda time to study both girls. While Crystal's dyed blond hair and perfect make-up were definitely meant to impress any male within range, Jennifer's long brown hair was pulled back in a ponytail and her freshly scrubbed face carried only a hint of lip gloss.

Hateful glances passed from Crystal to Jennifer. In contrast, Jennifer looked as though she only wanted to be friends with the girl who thought herself superior in every way.

"We were told you were Sean's date for the homecoming dance," Rhonda said, opening the conversation with Jennifer. "Were you dating prior to the dance?"

"Oh, no, Mrs. Pohs. I've never dated anyone. Mom says I can date, but I'm not pretty enough for any of the boys to be interested in me. When they are, all they talk about is what they want to do in bed. I don't want that, so I don't like to even talk to them."

"So, why did you go out with Sean?"

"Sean's a gentleman. He wasn't dating anyone and thought it was only right for the whole senior class to vote on who should be the queen. I knew I didn't have a chance of making it, but I did vote for myself."

"Why didn't you think you had a chance?" Phil questioned.

"Because I'm not as pretty as the other girls on the court. They're all cheerleaders and very popular. Of course, they couldn't run because they already had dates. There were only a few girls in the class who weren't dating. I guess that's why I won."

"How did you feel about your daughter being homecoming queen, Mr. Riley?"

Ted Riley looked up for the first time, his expression one of mixed emotions. "I knew it was something Jen wanted, but I was afraid those other girls on the court would make her feel less than special. You saw how Crystal Davis acted today. She's so jealous of not being homecoming queen, it's almost consuming her. I don't want Jen to become like her."

Rhonda knew exactly what Ted meant. "Was it like that for you on the court, Jennifer?"

Jennifer shook her head. "Only with Crystal. I think she didn't like the idea of Sean dancing with me all night and us having our picture taken for the yearbook as well as the newspaper. I don't think she liked being stuck with Mike, but he's been her boyfriend all summer and telling him to get lost is hard for her. She's the kind of girl who doesn't like to be without a guy in her life. Sean was only gone a few days last summer when Crystal started going out with Mike."

Phil and Rhonda both nodded in unison. This young girl was very intuitive about human nature. She'd pegged Crystal perfectly, but this gave no further insight into Sean's murder.

"Did you know about Sean's plans to take his grandfather's place on Halloween?" Phil asked, repeating the question asked to Crystal earlier.

"We talked on the phone several times after the dance," Jennifer confessed. "It wasn't like we were dating, but we seemed to have become good friends. He told me about his grandfather being very sick and how he wanted to carry on the Halloween tradition for him. I told him I thought it was a very caring gesture. I wish I'd never encouraged him. Sean was one of the most sincere and caring people I've ever met or hope to meet in my life."

"Do you have any idea who would have wanted to see Sean dead?"

Jennifer looked down at her folded hands and didn't try to stem the flow of tears from her eyes.

"It's okay, honey," her mother said. "Whatever you say here is going to stay in this room."

"Sean was elected captain of the football team last spring, before he left for South Dakota. When he came back and everyone found out about his Sioux heritage, a lot of the guys were unhappy about a half-breed being the captain of their all-American football team. It wasn't like he was different from before he went out to South Dakota. His appearance was the same, but when he looked into your eyes, it was like he could look into your very soul. In a way it was kind of creepy and yet it gave me a lot of peace. He looked at me as if I really mattered. It wasn't because I was pretty like the girls on the cheerleading squad, or I was smart. He seemed to be seeing me as a real person and someone he wanted to get to know better."

"Do you think anyone in your class is capable of doing something like this?"

Jennifer shook her head. "I don't want to think so. They were jealous of him, but I can't see anyone going so far as to kill him."

They talked for a few more minutes before Rhonda thanked the Rileys for taking the time to come in and talk to them.

"Those were two interesting conversations," Phil observed once they were alone in the conference room.

"I wish we would have videotaped both of them," Rhonda replied. "The audio tape will give us the responses, but I wish we had a video of those girls' facial expressions. Crystal is nothing more than a spoiled brat. Have you seen that show on TV, *Jerseylicious*?"

"My daughter likes to watch it, but I told her if she went that extreme with her make-up, I'd pull her in the bathroom and scrub it off myself. You know how kids are. She's only thirteen and wants to be thirty. If I were to choose a mentor for her, it would be someone like Jennifer rather than Crystal."

"I know what you mean. I remember girls like her in my class. They changed their hair color like I changed my underwear. One of the girls did it so often her hair actually turned green and started to fall out. It was really frightening."

"Whatever happened to her?"

"The last I heard, she married a guy from our class because she got pregnant. After a few years, he caught her turning tricks in the parking lot of the plant while he was at work. He divorced her and got full custody. From that disaster, she had two more kids by two more guys and married one of them. Of course, that ended in another divorce. The word is she's married to someone else now, but who knows how long that will last?"

"Do you think that's what will happen to Crystal?"

"It's possible, but unfortunately, she's looking for someone just like Daddy. Mike seems to fit the bill. She wants someone to completely dominate her. Even though she's a flirt, I doubt she's someone who will be the type to cheat on 'the man' in her life."

"Do you think she had anything to do with the murder?"

"I'm leaving that option open. I'm not sure she has what it takes to plan and execute a murder."

Phil agreed. "My money is on the football team. How many of them are seniors?"

"Let's go back to my office and check out the class roster."

Rhonda scanned the names of the seniors, matching them with those of the football team and cheerleading squad. "Let's see, we have Max Cleary and we know he's always been Sean's best friend. I think we need to talk to Mike Yankton, since he seems to be upset about Sean flaunting his Native American heritage. That leaves Doug Martin and Adam Banks. The remainder of the players are juniors. We can always call them in later if need be."

"I have the list of cheerleaders. Crystal Davis is the only senior who was on the court."

"That doesn't surprise me. The court is made up of the senior players and their dates. I doubt most of those guys would be interested in girls their own age when there are a lot of hot juniors and sophomores out there."

Phil nodded. "I'm old, but not ancient. I do remember high school. I certainly didn't want to date any of the girls in my class. They were familiar, the girls I'd known since kindergarten. Now the girls from the lower classes were something else. They represented the unknown and I really liked getting to know them."

"Point taken. I know the cheerleaders are usually the most beautiful girls in school, but I'd like to check out the dates for the other three seniors on the court. It's entirely possible they could be one of the younger girls on the squad."

Rhonda sorted through the mound of evidence they'd taken from the school, including the pictures taken at the homecoming dance a month earlier. The members of the court were easily identified. As king, Sean beamed under the metal crown studded with real-looking jewels. Next to Sean stood Max Cleary, Mike Yankton, Doug Martin, Adam Banks John Meisner and Wally Adams. On the other side of the line making up the court were the girls. Queen Jennifer Riley stood next to Sean with Annette Williams, Crystal Davis, Janice Stephens, Clarice Evans, Marie Gonzalez and Yvette King making up the remainder of the court.

She made a note of the names and divided the list between herself and Phil. While she contacted the families of the girls, Phil would be talking to those of the young men who not only played football with Sean, but also had been his classmates since kindergarten. They would both be in on the meetings with teenagers and parents, making both the girls and the boys feel more at ease.

By quitting time, each of the members of the court had been given an appointment for the following week. Their parents would accompany those who were under the age of eighteen, while the ones who were of age would be coming in on their own. The only opposition they found came from Mike Yankton. His parents wanted to come in with him to protect his interests even though he would be turning nineteen by the end of the year. Phil finally relented and said they could come in, but only to make Mike feel more at ease. They wouldn't be there to intervene for him, since he was legally an adult.

Chapter Ten

After church on Sunday morning, Rhonda insisted she and Mark stop at Nancy's home to see her again before she left for South Dakota.

Richard met them at the door. His smile was so genuine Rhonda got the impression he had expected to find her on Nancy's doorstep.

"It's good to see you again, Richard," Rhonda said. "I was afraid you'd leave before we could meet again."

"We will meet again. There is no doubt of that. I do not envy you the task before you. Sean's spirit has been speaking to me. He still does not know if the bullet that took his life was meant for him or for his grandfather."

The older man's words were not the ones Rhonda wanted to hear. Nevertheless, she knew they were the most sincere she'd heard since this all began over a week ago.

"Do the spirits speak to you often?" Mark asked, a tone of awe and wonder in his voice.

"It is not something I can control, if that is what you want to know. Being here I can only communicate with Sean. Once I return to my home, I will again be able to regain contact with the ancestors."

"Do you think they'll be able to tell you who did this?" Rhonda questioned, hoping against hope for any help she could get with this investigation.

"What you are looking for is not an exact science. Being able to make contact with the spirits is a practice as ancient as time itself. I learned how to be a shaman from my father and his father before him. My son, Nancy's uncle, has learned his lessons well, but he has had a lifetime to perfect his craft. No matter how long he and his son study, they do not possess the knowledge Sean portrayed. He outshined anyone our people have had with us since before the time of Sitting Bull and

Crazy Horse. He was destined for great things until the ancestors told me the ancients needed him more than the people."

"Do you really believe that?" Mark inquired.

Richard nodded his head. "It is hard for me to explain. This is our culture. It is something we are born to, something instilled in us since birth."

"I really don't understand," Rhonda said. "Until last summer no one around here even knew of his heritage."

"What you don't understand is as soon as Sean came to be with us, the ancestors recognized him as a very old soul. The ancients made it clear his knowledge is needed in the council of elders. No matter what god we worship, we all know on the day of our birth the moment of our death is known and nothing we can do or say can change it."

Rhonda pondered Richard's words. She remembered her grandfather telling her he wished he knew when he was going to die, where he was going to be and what he was going to be doing, so he could be somewhere else, doing something else on that day. This saying came back to haunt her several times during her life. It wasn't that she was a fatalist, she didn't try to take unnecessary chances, but she did know God numbered our days at the moment of our birth.

"I thought I heard voices down here," Nancy said as she entered the room. "I was doing some last minute packing and cleaning before we leave tomorrow and the renters move in."

"I know this must be a very difficult decision for you to make, but I'm certain you will be in good hands staying with your grandparents. I only wish I could have met your grandmother."

"You'd love her, but she hasn't been well for several months. In a way my going out there will be a blessing since I'll be able to take care of her. Maybe I'll even find I have some of the intuitiveness Sean found last summer. I've never explored my heritage before. I think this is something Sean would want me to do."

Rhonda wondered if Nancy's upbeat mood was an act or something she thought was expected of her.

"Were you able to talk to Crystal and Jennifer?" Nancy finally asked, changing the subject.

"Yes, we were, but we're not at liberty to disclose anything that was said."

"I understand. I wish I'd gotten to know Jennifer better. She seemed like such a down-to-earth young woman when I met her at the homecoming dance. I went there for the presentation of the court and to get some pictures of Sean being crowned king.

"I'm not sure if I know the names of all the kids. At least I can't remember them," Nancy said. "Do you think you can give me the names of each couple so I can write them on the back?" She picked up a packet of pictures and handed them to Rhonda.

At a loss, Rhonda turned to Mark. "Let's see," Mark began. "There's Sean and Jennifer, of course. This is Max Cleary and Annette Williams, Mike Yankton and Crystal Davis, Doug Martin and Janice Stephens, Adam Banks and Clarice Evans, John Meisner and Marie Gonzales, and Wally Adams and Yvette King," Mark said, identifying each couple from the court.

"Was it your idea to take pictures of all the couples on the court?" Rhonda asked.

"No, it was Sean's idea. He said they'd been playing football together for more years than any of them wanted to admit and this would be the last football related thing they would be doing. These boys were his best friends. He knew most of them were going off to college and up until last summer, he thought he'd be doing the same thing. Going out to visit my grandparents was the best thing that could have happened to him. For the first time in his life, he knew what he wanted to do with his life."

Across the room, Rhonda saw Richard sit down on one of the straight chairs and put his head in his hand.

"All is not as it seems," he said, his voice not sounding anything like it did moments earlier.

Rhonda looked from Nancy to Mark and was shocked to see the color drain from both of their faces.

"Sean?" Nancy questioned, her voice hardly louder than a hoarse whisper.

Rhonda felt her legs go weak. *Could the voice coming from*

Richard's mouth be that of Sean from beyond the grave?

"Sean?" Nancy repeated as she grasped the back of the sofa for support.

Her plaintive wail, coupled with desperate sobs, seemed to have broken Richard's trance. Before their eyes, his expression changed and he looked as though he was unaware of what had just transpired.

~ * ~

"What just happened in there?" Mark asked as they headed for home. "Do you think Sean's spirit spoke to us?"

Rhonda sat for a moment, contemplating her answer. "There are a lot of things about the Native American culture I don't understand. I've heard about shamans going into trances and communicating with spirits. I just didn't think I'd ever see it for myself. I couldn't identify the voice as belonging to Sean, but what was said makes me wonder what else will be revealed."

"Well, I can identify the voice. It was Sean. I'd be willing to bet anything you want on it. I doubt Richard could fake it. His natural speaking voice is too low to be able to pull off Sean's higher-pitched tenor."

"That said, I'm completely baffled."

"Is there something about this you want to talk about?"

Mark's question put Rhonda in the middle of an emotional tug of war. "I wish I could. For one thing, you're involved in this deeper than you realize. For another, what I'm finding is privileged information. To be truthful, we're going to have to start questioning the football team and after what just happened, I think we have to start with you tomorrow morning."

Mark pulled into the driveway and turned to face Rhonda. "You don't think I'm involved in this, do you?"

"Not in the way you think. There are certain things that have come to light and there are questions that have to be answered before we can get to the truth." She could tell by the look on Mark's face he was as concerned as she.

"Something tells me you need some time alone. I'll go down to Subway and get us some sandwiches for lunch. What else would you like?"

"No chips, we have those here. We also have soda, but I'd really like some of those macadamia nut cookies."

"Your wish is my command, lovely lady. I'll be back in forty-five minutes. Will that give you enough time?"

She stood at the front door, watching as Mark pulled out of the driveway. Once he turned the corner, she slipped her key into the lock and entered the house. Going into the downstairs office, she placed a call to Phil.

"What's wrong, Rhonda?" Phil asked.

She began to explain what happened at Nancy's house less than an hour ago. "I think we have to step up our investigation of the football team, starting with Mark, the first thing tomorrow morning."

"Mark? Why would we start with your husband?"

"Because he's the coach of the team. He knows more of what is going on than anyone might think. I'm sure he doesn't even know how much information he picks up in the locker room."

"What about that stuff IT is working on for us?"

"We both know that could take longer than either of us thinks. We have to look at every avenue to solve this one. We owe it to Sean, to say nothing of his family."

She'd just hung up the phone when Mark returned with their lunch. Tomorrow's interview hung between them, something not mentioned and yet on both of their minds.

"So what did you bring me?" she asked, trying to sound like an excited child rather than a concerned detective.

"You know me. I'm a creature of habit. I got us each a cold cut combo with all the fixings. As usual, I put cheese on mine but not yours and I skipped the peppers on both of them."

Rhonda could feel her mouth begin to water. It wasn't often they had subs, but when they did, this one was her favorite. While Mark unpacked the bag, Rhonda got out the fruit salad they'd had for dinner the previous night and opened a soda for each of them.

"Did I give you enough time?"

"More than enough."

Before they could begin eating, Rhonda's cell phone rang. Nancy was the last person Rhonda expected to receive a call from.

"I just had word from the hospital. John passed away early this morning. I won't be leaving for South Dakota until after the funeral."

"I'm so sorry. Is there anything we can do?"

There was an awkward pause in the conversation. "I don't know how to ask this, but Beverly is afraid of what might happen at the visitation and the funeral. She wanted me to ask if you could be at both of them?"

"Of course I can. When are they planned?"

"I doubt much can be done before Tuesday night and Wednesday, but I'll have to let you know the details for certain. I told Beverly I'd meet her at the funeral home. I know when I tell her you will be with us it will put her mind at ease."

"More problems?" Mark asked as Rhonda hung up the phone and turned her attention to the sandwich in front of her.

"I'm afraid so. John Richardson passed away this morning. I'm afraid his Halloween tradition has come to an end. Instead of all the joy it brought him in the past, it now represents only tragedy."

Chapter Eleven

Monday morning Rhonda waited for Mark to arrive. She never thought she'd be interrogating her husband, but the way this investigation was going, she had no other option.

"I'm only letting you sit in on this one because you're the primary on the case, Rhonda," Sheriff Cantwell advised. "I don't really approve of you questioning your husband but since it was your suggestion, I would like to have Phil do the talking."

Rhonda agreed. She certainly didn't want to question Mark, but so much of the information they'd uncovered pointed to the football team, she realized they needed to start with the one member of the high school faculty who knew the kids best.

Mark arrived on time and together with Phil went into the conference room where two days earlier they'd talked to Crystal and Jennifer.

"Do you know why we called you in today, Mark?" Phil asked as his opening question.

Mark shook his head. "Not really. You know my wife. When she's on a case, especially this case, she's very tightlipped."

"To begin with, let me tell you everything we say here is being recorded. We don't want you to have any surprises. We know Sean was made captain of the football team last spring. From what we've learned, after he revealed his Native American heritage, there was some talk about replacing him."

Rhonda watched Mark's expression to Phil's statement.

"It all goes back to that gal who pitched such a fit a few years back about the team not being called the War Hawks with the Indian mascot. Of course, it wasn't just here but all over the state. The last I heard, they're debating this in almost every part of the country."

"Did you hear anything about Sean being replaced as captain because of his heritage?"

"You know how kids are. Once they found out where Sean spent the summer and that he was considering ditching college to go back, there was some grousing from the guys. Mike and Adam both said things about if Indian mascots weren't going to be allowed, why should a half-breed be allowed to play? There was some support from the juniors, but in the end the majority of the seniors overruled them and Sean continued on as their captain."

"What kind of feedback have you had from the team since the funeral?"

"These guys talk a good show, but they're all broken up about this. Everyone at school looks up to them as role models and tough guys at the same time. In fact, they're just kids and adjusting to the loss of a classmate is hard, especially when it happens in such a violent way."

"Why do you think Mike and Adam were so adamant about Sean's heritage?" Sheriff Cantwell asked, joining the questioning for the first time.

"Back when all the flap about the mascot was going on, their dads were the most vocal about it. If you ask me, those guys would have made great skinheads when they were younger. I'm sure they tolerate the black kids on the team, but they have one solid hatred for Native Americans, especially ones who have left the reservations and made something of their lives. I'm sure they were more than a little upset to find out about Sean's family."

"Do you know what's behind this?"

"I wish I did. I just remember those two guys saying they agreed about the mascot, not because they thought it was degrading to the Indians, but because they didn't want them to be glorified. They used a lot of hateful words back then and called them mindless savages and other things that weren't so nice. I'm sure their ideas rubbed off on their kids."

Rhonda looked at her hurriedly jotted notes, realizing she would be the only one who could make sense out of her makeshift shorthand.

"Can I ask a question?" Mark inquired.

"Of course you can," Rhonda assured him.

"Do you think someone on the football team could be behind this?"

Sheriff Cantwell looked Mark directly in the eye. "We have no idea who is and who isn't involved. We're just exploring every option at this point. The way we see it, the members of the football team were some of Sean's closest friends. It's only logical they might know something, no matter how trivial, that could help us."

The tension of the comment held in the air of the room, making Rhonda uneasy. She wished she hadn't asked to be in on this interview, but hindsight was always twenty-twenty.

"Going back a bit," Phil finally said. "Just how involved were Dan Yankton and Steve Banks in this school mascot thing?"

Mark took a moment, as though thinking about the answer Phil's question required. "They were very involved, but not in the same way as it was originally intended."

"I don't understand," Sheriff Cantwell commented. "Are you trying to confuse the issue?"

"I don't mean for it to be confusing," Mark continued. "The original concept was the fact that the comic-like images of the Native American mascots were demeaning. I never thought they were, but people all over the state seemed to agree. Unfortunately, Dan and Steve took it one step further. They started a rant about how our students and athletes shouldn't be equated to the dirty, murdering savages."

"Are you saying they're racists?"

"Not in the way you might think. Like I said earlier, we have black students on each of our sports teams and they seem to have no problem with them, but get them talking about Native Americans and it's a whole other issue. Until Sean told everyone about his family on his mother's side, there was no conflict. If we were up north and closer to the area where they actually have reservations, they might be justified in the prejudice. Around here, such things just aren't a problem."

"Were either of the fathers involved in this business of the team wanting Sean removed as team captain?"

Again Mark took a moment to consider his answer. "I didn't have any dealings with either of them. I heard what the kids were saying and tried to defuse the situation. Fortunately, the team members in favor of Sean being the captain of the football team overruled Mike and Adam as well as their followers."

Rhonda's mind spun. Her suspect list for this case seemed to be growing by leaps and bounds. Now, not only did she need to talk to football players and cheerleaders, she had to contend with bigoted parents as well as the unknown person who'd sent John the e-mail.

It was almost noon when the interview finally ended. One question led to another, bringing more and more suspects to light. Even though Rhonda hadn't asked any of the questions, she felt completely drained by the time they wrapped everything up.

"Why don't you and Mark go and get some lunch?" Phil suggested. "When you get back, you can help me get started on calling in football team members and cheerleaders."

"Just be sure to bring in the parents of the ones who are under eighteen," Mark cautioned. "I know not only the kids but also their folks, and there'll be hell to pay if you don't."

Phil laughed. "There's no way in hell I'd do anything like that after the confrontation we had with Vern Davis on Saturday. I think Rhonda will agree with me when I say we'll bring in the parents of all of them, no matter what their age. I've had nightmares about that guy all weekend." Mark turned to face Phil. "Did you say Vern Davis?" Phil nodded.

"As I recall, he is one of Dan's cronies. He's always been vocal about Native Americans. He once said it was because he grew up close to one of the reservations in Oklahoma. It's his contention all Indians are lazy bastards. I try to steer clear of the three of them, since I don't like such discussions. I figured the reason Crystal started dating Mike last summer was because Sean went to spend the summer on a reservation in South Dakota."

Before going out to lunch with Mark, Rhonda returned to her office to leave her notes from the morning's meeting. After what Mark and Phil just said, she needed a moment away from everything that was happening around her.

"I know I'm not under suspicion," Mark said while they waited for their lunch to be delivered to their table. "I can only imagine how intense things could get if you thought I had a hand in this."

"You know you aren't a suspect," Rhonda assured him. "Being the coach for these kids, you know them probably better than their parents. Everything you told us today has been helpful. I just don't relish having to deal with such a large number of teenagers."

Mark laughed at her comment, breaking the tension between them. "It's a good thing you didn't become a teacher."

~ * ~

Rhonda returned to her desk and settled into making calls to set up appointments with the girls on the cheerleading squad. Having already talked to Crystal Davis, her next call was placed to Janice Stephens, the junior from the squad who was on the homecoming court. Thankfully, the parents of each girl she called were more than willing to come in with their daughters.

The first appointment was made with Janice and her parents. They arrived promptly at three-thirty. "I don't know what Janice can tell you," Mrs. Stephens protested.

Rhonda sat down across the table from Janice and tried to put both parents and daughter at ease. "I saw the pictures of Doug and you at the dance. You make a good looking couple."

Janice beamed at the compliment.

"As a member of the homecoming court, did you hear any talk about Sean and his date?"

"No one was happy about Jen being queen. You have to know we weren't all cheerleaders, but at least we're part of the popular crowd. Sean couldn't find a bigger nerd if he tried. She's the girl who walks into class and screws up the grading curve."

"I've checked Annette Williams and Marie Gonzalez and they aren't cheerleaders. Did you have a problem with them being on the court?"

"That's different. Annette and Max have been dating for a year and a half. John and Marie are going steady and it's the same with Wally and Yvette. Jen's nice enough, but she doesn't belong. If Sean hadn't told everyone he was a half breed, he would have been able to get a date with someone acceptable. If he hadn't gone off to play Indian last summer, Crystal would have been queen. She deserved that much for dating him so long without knowing what he really was."

"Janice! What a thing to say," Mrs. Stephens declared. A look of disbelief crossed her face as though she had no idea what her daughter was talking about.

"Well, it's the truth. We all knew Sean would be made captain of the football team and that would make him the king of homecoming. Everything would have been all right if Sean hadn't gone away last summer."

Rhonda took a deep breath. Mark was right; it was a good thing she hadn't become a teacher. She had no idea how anyone could put up with teenage drama on a daily basis.

"From the pictures Mrs. Richardson took at the dance, it looks like all of you had a good time, even if Crystal wasn't the queen. To be truthful, I don't think the homecoming dance had anything to do with Sean's death two weeks later. The problem is someone planned this murder. Do you have any idea of anyone who could have planned such a thing?"

"I—I," Janice started to cry, "I don't think so. I mean Crystal and Mike said he was nothing but a lazy dirty savage, but it was just trash talk."

Mr. and Mrs. Stephens looked as though they could hardly wait to get their daughter home. Rhonda was certain they'd never heard Janice talk in such a crude manner.

Rhonda finished her interview and went back to her office where Phil waited for her. "How did your meeting with the Stephens girl go?"

"I know there's a reason I don't want to have children. We've just uncovered the tip of the iceberg on this one. How did you do with Doug Martin?"

"He's not as racist as I thought he'd be. I'm not looking forward to talking to Adam Banks and Mike Yankton tomorrow, to say nothing of dealing with Steve and Dan. It's been a long day. I'm more than ready to go home. We've got more appointments set for tomorrow, to say nothing of John's visitation at night."

Rhonda agreed and checked her e-mail one more time before calling it a day. To her surprise, one of the messages came from Nancy Richardson and contained an attachment filled with the pictures from the homecoming dance. She should have asked for copies on Sunday, but when Richard went into the trance and spoke in Sean's voice, she'd completely forgotten to ask for them.

She made a note to herself to have IT make copies of them. For now, it was time to call it a day.

Chapter Twelve

By three, Rhonda had talked to three more of the cheerleaders as well as their parents. The general consensus was that none of the girls shed any further light on the investigation.

She could have set more appointments, but tonight was John's visitation and she wanted to be one of the first people to arrive. Not only had she promised Nancy she'd be there, but also John was as much a part of this investigation as Sean.

Entering the funeral home, Rhonda thought back to the flower-filled viewing room and closed casket of Sean's visitation just over a week earlier.

After signing the guest book, she stepped into the room. A photo array set to music, played out on the several flat screen televisions mounted around the room. Although the floral arrangements weren't as numerous, the theme running through all of them sent a chill through Rhonda's body.

The casket spray had a scarecrow with a pumpkin head set in the center of the flowers. In many of the other arrangements, small scarecrows peeked out through mums, dahlias and other fall flowers as well as the artificial arrangements. Even with the horrific connotation of the scarecrow and its connection to Sean's death, she knew the tradition was something enjoyed and looked forward to over the years. With John's passing and the tragedy of the drive by shooting on Halloween, Rhonda knew the tradition would die with its founder.

She made her way through the receiving line made up of children and grandchildren. As she did, she mouthed the words of condolences she hoped sounded appropriate until she reached Beverly. "I'm so sorry," she said as she embraced the older woman.

"This is what John wanted. The doctors told us months ago he didn't have much time left and death was inevitable. He told the doctor he wanted to be the scarecrow one more time. It broke his heart when they told him he couldn't sit out there. I wasn't even going to hand out candy this year, but Sean said it wouldn't be right and he wanted to take his grandfather's place. John was so proud of him." She started to cry and wiped at her eyes with the lace-edged handkerchief she held in her hand.

Rhonda knew there was nothing more she could say to ease Beverly's pain. Instead, she moved on and spotted Nancy sitting with her grandfather on one of the couches provided for the mourners who were not standing in the receiving line.

"Why aren't you with the rest of the family?" Rhonda asked.

"My daughter is with her cousins, but I didn't feel comfortable with the rest of them. Although I got along well with John and Beverly, Hank's brothers and sisters never really approved of me. I was so different from them with my dark hair and brown eyes, I never felt like I belonged. After everything that's happened, I'm more of an outsider than ever."

Rhonda nodded. She couldn't fault Nancy for her feelings. For the third time in a year, she was burying a close male member of her family. It had to be hard to be in her position. By marriage, she was like a daughter to John and Beverly, but to the rest of the family she was an 'in-law,' someone who never really belonged.

"They are all together now," Rhonda said, holding Nancy's hand consolingly.

Richard looked directly into Rhonda's eyes. "Sean tells me he and his father welcomed John with open arms. It is as it was meant to be."

Rhonda wanted to stay and talk longer, but the lump in her throat prevented it. From the corner of her eye, she saw Chuck Hadley, the funeral director, motioning her to join him.

"Is there something I can do for you, Chuck?" she asked once she was out of the visitation area.

"I have something I'd like to have you look at. You know we get all kinds of floral arrangements, but what we found at the front door just prior to the beginning of the visitation really scared me. I figured you'd be here, so there was no need to call in the police, so I had it moved to one of the storage rooms so it wouldn't upset the family."

"Don't tell me you..."

"Of course we didn't get fingerprints all over it," Chuck interrupted. "We used latex gloves and moved it very carefully."

Rhonda followed Chuck out of the reception hallway and into a storage area. In one corner of the room stood a rocking chair with a scarecrow looking like John sitting there with the pumpkin head pitched forward. The front of the pumpkin was shattered as though it had suffered a bullet wound. The red plaid flannel shirt was soaked with fake blood.

As though she were in a movie, flashes of Sean lying on the porch with the shell of the shattered pumpkin still around his neck and blood staining the front of his shirt from the head wound, took the place of the gruesome scene before her eyes. For an instant, her knees threatened to buckle and no longer support her weight.

"Are you all right?" Chuck asked, as he put his arm around her shoulders to support her sagging body.

"This is just too creepy. Who would send something like this, considering all the family has been through?" Rhonda didn't expect an answer to her question. She knew, all too well, it could have only come from one person and that had to be the murderer. "Was—was there a card?" She finally managed to ask.

Before Chuck could answer, she looked down to see a card clutched in the white canvas-clad hand of the scarecrow.

"Don't touch it. I'll make a call and have the forensic team come over here. We need pictures of this and everything has to be dusted for fingerprints. Is there a back door they can use to get into this room? I certainly don't want to alert the family to anything being amiss. They've been through enough these past couple of weeks."

Chuck nodded toward a curtain. "That's an outside door. We use it to bring in the bodies to prepare them for burial. This room leads directly into the preparation area. There's a garage attached in the back. If you call in your team, we'll have the door open for them. No one will even know they're here."

Still shaken, Rhonda went back out into the hallway before placing a call to the forensic department of the sheriff's office. "Can you send someone over to the Hadley Funeral Home? Have them come around to the back and come in through the garage. The door will be open. Text me when they get here."

She slipped the phone back into the pocket of her jacket and contemplated the terrible sight of the arrangement that had so mysteriously appeared at the funeral home door earlier in the day.

"I thought you'd be in monitoring conversations."

Rhonda tuned at the sound of Phil's voice. She knew he'd be here tonight, but not seeing him before he spoke caused her insides to jump as though she'd been shot. "I—I was," she stammered. "There's been a new development. I've called the forensic team in."

"New development? What? Where?"

"Shhh. Not so loud. There was a macabre arrangement delivered here this afternoon. Chuck had it put in the storage room so no one would be upset by it. The problem is, I don't know if I can look at the thing again. That's why I turned it over to forensic."

"Can I see it?"

Before Rhonda could answer, her phone rang, indicating she had a text message. Looking at the screen, she saw the note saying the forensic team was outside the garage door and needed it to be opened for them.

Leaving Phil with more questions than answers, Rhonda went to find Chuck. "Didn't you open that garage door?" she asked in a low whisper.

"I'm sorry, something came up and I forgot. I'll go and do it now."

"Then take Phil with you. I don't know if I can take looking at that thing again."

Chuck nodded and motioned for Phil to follow him. Once they headed toward the storage room, Rhonda went back into the viewing room and sat down, too shaken to even speak with anyone.

How long she sat alone she didn't know, but as silently as he had at Sean's funeral, Richard joined her. "Your soul is troubled," he said, startling her with his silent approach and presence. "Do you want to talk to me about it?"

Why she said anything to Richard, she didn't know, but somehow she knew telling him about the grotesque thing she'd just seen was as natural as talking to anyone in the department about the case.

"Do you think I would be allowed to see this thing that has you so upset?"

In her mind, she knew she shouldn't allow this to happen, but her heart told her it was the right thing to do. If anyone could understand the strange meaning of this, it would be him. "You have to promise you won't tell anyone about this and you can't touch anything, but with your connection to the spirit world, maybe you can make sense of it."

She'd just gotten to her feet when she saw Phil enter the room and motion for her to join him in the hallway.

"Is something wrong?" Rhonda asked, when along with Richard she joined Phil in the hallway.

"It's something I think you need to see," Phil replied, looking skeptically at Richard.

"It's all right, Phil. I told Richard about what we found. He wants to see it for himself. Considering his connection to the spirit world, I think he may be able to help us."

Richard turned and faced Phil. "I can understand your concerns. I do not mean to do anything to compromise your investigation of Sean's murder. Possibly if I tell you about what Rhonda wanted to show me and what the card attached to it says, you will be more comfortable with me coming with you."

"How would you know what the card says?"

"I asked Rhonda what was wrong and while she was telling me, the spirit of my great-grandson came to me and said the card would not be signed and it would read—rest in peace, pumpkin head."

Rhonda watched as the color drained from Phil's face. "That's exactly what it says. I don't know how you did it; that is, unless you sent it."

"To the contrary, I did not send it and knew nothing about it until

I talked to Rhonda. I only know the contents of the note because of the will of the spirits. We are not the only ones who want this crime solved. The ancestors are very concerned because although Sean is happy with them, his soul is troubled because of the way he died."

"You can believe Richard when he says he had nothing to do with sending *that* thing," Rhonda said, more than a bit perturbed by Phil's accusation.

"I agree with you, but you have to agree it's uncanny when something no one knows but the forensic team and myself is told to us by anyone else."

"Then you don't mind if I take Richard in to see it?" Rhonda asked.

"I don't have to remind you that you're the primary on this case. This is your call."

Although she knew she would catch flak from her superiors for involving a civilian in her investigation, she decided Richard's opinion on this strange thing would be invaluable.

With trepidation, she walked into the storage room just ahead of Richard and Phil. The impact of the arrangement was not as bad as she originally felt it to be. This time she saw other aspects of it. Along with the scarecrow was a corn shock and at the base of the rocking chair stood pots of brightly colored mums. Whoever brought this to the funeral home had gone to a great expense to get their message across. She wondered if it was meant to tell her by questioning the members of the football team and cheerleading squad she was looking in the wrong direction.

"I sense evil in this," Richard said. "The ancestors tell me this person is looking for recognition."

"Are you saying he wants to be caught?" Phil asked.

"I never said *he*. The person behind this is watching everything very closely. Whoever it is does not want to be caught. They are enjoying this game of cat and mouse they are playing with you. All will come to light when the time is right, but not before. I am afraid that is all the ancestors have revealed to me."

~ * ~

Hours later, Rhonda left the funeral home completely drained. She had not been able to concentrate on the individuals paying their respects to John's family. The strange arrangement that had been left at the front door of the funeral home drove all thoughts of duty from her mind. "You look drained," Mark said, when she returned home.

"Did you learn anything new tonight?"

Rhonda thought about confiding in Mark, but decided against it. "Not really. It's just been a very long day. I think I'll just take a nice hot bath and head for bed."

"I thought that's how you might feel. I drew a bath for you when I heard the garage door go up. When you're done, I have a light snack for us and then I'll give you a massage. Maybe that will relieve some of your tension."

She smiled at her husband. He knew her so well, right down to the fact she'd skipped supper in order to get to the visitation before it started at four this afternoon. Now, after eight, he realized she needed not only to relax but also to eat.

Chapter Thirteen

Rhonda could hardly wait to read the report from the forensic team regarding the strange arrangement sent to the funeral home. The report she expected to find on her desk wasn't there. Instead, Sheriff Cantwell waited for her.

"It sounds like you had a very interesting night at the funeral home," he said.

The muscles in her stomach began to clinch. Last night she acted on her impulses without any thought for the ramifications. This morning, the thing she worried about the most stood in her office, ready to condemn her for her actions. "Interesting isn't a strong enough word," she began, trying to keep her voice calm when her head was spinning and her stomach churning. "I'm sure you heard about me bringing Richard Brave Beaver in to see the arrangement. In my defense..."

Her superior silenced her with a wave of his hand. "In your position I would have done the same thing. This is a tough case. I've never seen a murder case that was easy. I have just one question. Did you actually see the card attached to the arrangement?"

Rhonda shook her head. "No, I didn't. By the time Phil and I went into the room, the forensic team was already in the process of bagging it. I only knew what it said because Richard told me, and Phil confirmed it."

"Would you be surprised to know Phil didn't see it either?"

Rhonda knew the expression on her face had to be one of shock.

"He only knew what the forensics people told him. He was as surprised as you were when Richard confirmed it word for word. Richard continues to amaze me, so I wondered why he hadn't been able to see the rest of the message. What he could *see* were only the words that were relevant to John and Sean. There was another message printed on the inside of the envelope. It wasn't found until everything came back to the lab."

"Why not?"

"Because no one was looking for it. I think it's for the best if we go in to the conference room for the meeting with the forensic team."

Rhonda checked her watch. It was only a little after nine. She hoped this wouldn't take too long. She didn't want to miss John's funeral at noon, but her interest in what was found last night had been piqued. Maybe something would come to light to blow the lid off this case.

Phil waited for her in the conference room, along with two men and a woman Rhonda recognized from the day shift of the lab. She could read nothing in their expressions to give her any idea of what they learned.

"Good, we're all here," Melinda Carter from the lab said once they were all seated. "The arrangement that was delivered to the funeral home yesterday afternoon was very interesting. It was a message to Rhonda rather than the family. It was meant to shock and frighten. Whoever sent it knew the family would never get a chance to see it."

"What do you mean?" Rhonda asked.

"Most of the stuff was pretty generic. The rocker was like the ones sitting on the porch at the Cracker Barrel Restaurant out by the highway. The mums came from Wal-Mart. The flannel shirt isn't a new one, so we're testing it for DNA. Last but not least, the pumpkin is like the ones on sale at Wal-Mart. We checked with the Cracker Barrel and they can account for all their rockers. Therefore, this one wasn't stolen. On further inspection, we found it wasn't purchased there and was a knock off. It was probably purchased at one of the discount stores from their garden shop last spring."

"So what does all this have to do with me?"

"I'm getting to that. We lifted some prints from the envelope that held the note, but we have nothing concrete to go on yet. The note was printed in black ink and read *Rest in Peace Pumpkin Head*. The guys last night only pulled it out far enough to read the note. When we took it completely out of the envelope this morning, we saw what was printed in red on the inside of the envelope. We photographed it."

Melinda handed Rhonda a blown up photograph. The printing was very tiny, but the message came across as bold and frightening. *It's so much fun to watch you squirm-Catch me if you can, Detective Pohs.*

Rhonda took a deep breath. "Who the hell is this guy?"

"I don't know," Sheriff Cantwell replied. "Are you sure you should go to that funeral today?"

Memories of the funerals she'd attended for the other murders she'd investigated crowded her mind. The first had been the most frightening, since someone attacked her with a rock. The next two had passed with no problems, but that didn't make them any odder. This one could turn weird as well, but that was a chance she had to take.

"I'm committed to this one. Besides, whoever is behind this is expecting to see me there. If I get lucky, someone might tip their hand. If I don't show up, this guy will think he's won and has scared us off."

"He has scared us, Rhonda." Cantwell said, "You're not going to the funeral alone. Phil and I will be there with you."

Rhonda nodded in agreement. Even though she expected no problems, it would be good to have them there to watch her back.

~ * ~

The church was filled with family and friends. Unlike Sean's funeral that had been overflowing with teenagers, the mourners were mostly retirees.

Everyone seemed to be genuinely in mourning over John's death. Even the comical little scarecrows in the arrangements did little to lighten the mood of the day.

At the cemetery, Rhonda expected Richard to do a chant in the same way he did at Sean's funeral. Instead, he stayed back to give comfort to Nancy who once again stood off by herself rather than join the rest of John's family.

"I'm so glad you came," Nancy said. "I was afraid I wouldn't see you again before I left in the morning. I'm so blessed that Grandfather could stay on with me until this funeral was over."

"I'm going to miss you," Rhonda replied, sincerely meaning the words she just said. Although she hadn't known Nancy before the murder, she'd learned to envy Nancy's strength throughout this ordeal. "Of course, I can understand your need to get away from everything here."

"I worried about leaving Beverly here with her memories, but her daughter, Alice, has persuaded her to come and stay with them in Madison for the winter. We talked about it last night after the visitation and all agreed it's for the best."

Rhonda pondered the meaning behind Nancy's words. Last night and again today Nancy had stood aside from the nucleus of the family. During those times, Rhonda had seen no attempt, on anyone's part, to draw the woman they'd called sister and daughter for over twenty years, into their midst. Before Rhonda could voice a biting response, Beverly joined them.

"I see your partner and the sheriff are both here. We'd like all of you to come back to the church for the luncheon. Since both Nancy and I are leaving town tomorrow, there are a lot of questions the family wants to ask."

Rhonda looked toward Sheriff Cantwell and Phil. They were engaged in conversation with Beverly's son, David. When she caught Phil's eye, he nodded to her, indicating they would all be going back to the church.

A light snow had started falling during the graveside service. One by one the mourners left for the protection of their vehicles. Following suit, Rhonda and Phil went with Sheriff Cantwell to their waiting unmarked county car.

"Did you notice anything out of the ordinary, Rhonda?" Sheriff Cantwell asked as they followed the line of cars going back toward town.

"Not really, but I did get a very uneasy feeling. Last night Nancy and her grandfather sat away from the family. It was the same today. I just don't understand it. She may no longer be married to Hank, but she's been part of that family for a long time. How can she suddenly be treated like a poor relative?"

"I gave up trying to understand family dynamics a long time ago. From what I've gathered, Hank was the only one of the kids who stayed in the area. David told me he went to college and ended up working in Green Bay. As for Steven, he is teaching school in Rockford and Alice and her husband live and work in Madison. Hank stayed here and helped with the farm work in addition to working at the bank in town. I think he was instrumental in the subdivision of the property. John was getting older and to continue working the land seemed out of the question."

"But that doesn't explain the way they were treating Nancy."

"That's one of the things I want to see if we can find out at the luncheon," Phil said. "I've found out she has been taking Beverly and John to all of their doctor appointments ever since Hank died. She gave up her job when Hank was sick and didn't go back to work. I think there was enough insurance and pension so she could live comfortably without working. It gave Beverly and John the perfect person to see to their needs. Now with Nancy saying she's going to South Dakota to try to make sense out of everything, the family must feel like she's deserting them."

They continued their discussion until at last they parked in the church lot. Rhonda hoped she could find a reason to shake her uneasiness about Nancy, as well as other things, before it was time to go back to work.

The warmth inside the fellowship hall of the church was welcome after the walk from the parking lot. Along with the snow, a brisk wind had come up, biting their cheeks with the sting of the snow along with the chill of the dropping temperature.

Long tables were set up with a bountiful buffet dominating the far end of the room. After filling their plates, they looked around to find empty chairs. Phil was motioned over to a table where Alice and Beverly were seated, while Sheriff Cantwell joined David, and Rhonda went to sit with Steven. It was obvious each of the family members wanted to have a private conversation with the police officers in attendance, one that didn't seem to include Nancy.

"Sean was my nephew," Steven said as they were finally seated and the minister said grace. "I loved him, you have to know that. We've all talked about it and are confused. Was the bullet that took his life meant for him or for our father? Do you have any leads?"

Rhonda swallowed hard. This was her case and yet there was nothing she could say since she had no concrete information. "As you know, the shooting was a drive-by with no apparent motive. The more we check into things, the more we think this was well planned. The problem is, who was the intended victim? When we drove by the house that night, I was certain it was John sitting on the porch. I had no idea he was in the hospital. I don't think many people knew how sick he was. As for Sean, he only told a few of his friends about taking his grandfather's place this year."

"Why do you think this was planned?" Steven's wife Tammy questioned.

"Because the car used in the drive-by was stolen from Clinton. It was found totaled and wiped completely clean of fingerprints hours after the shooting." Rhonda guarded what she said very closely. The information she was imparting to the family at this table was nothing that hadn't been reported in the paper and on the evening news many times over in the past week and a half.

"Well," Steve finally said, "if you want my opinion, I think Sean was the target of this shooting. We all knew about Nancy's Native American blood, but she never made a big deal out of it. Last summer, after Hank's death, Sean felt like he wanted to pursue it further. Things would have been a hell of a lot better if he'd kept his mouth shut about what went on out in South Dakota. He got on his soapbox and proclaimed he wanted to go to South Dakota and live on the reservation after graduation. After that mess about the school mascot a few years back, there's been a lot of talk about the Native Americans of this country, both pro and con. If you ask me, he brought this on himself."

Rhonda was stunned. How could this man be saying such things about his nephew? She could hardly wait for the luncheon to be over so she could compare notes with Sheriff Cantwell and Phil.

~ * ~

"I would certainly like to have had that conversation with David taped," Sheriff Cantwell said as they headed back toward the office. "I realize this family has been through a lot these past couple of years. I can't imagine losing first my brother and then my nephew and father. I remember when my nephew died of cancer. The whole family took it hard, but most of us have realized it was for the best. That's the way it was for John and Hank, but Sean's death was so senseless."

"I know what you mean," Phil commented. "Beverly was pretty much in shock over the whole thing, but Alice seems to be very vocal. I asked her why Nancy wasn't with the family in the receiving line last night. She said it was for the best. If it hadn't been for Sean's newfound vocation, maybe none of this would have happened. She also said if she'd known the extent of Sean's involvement with his great grandfather, she would have insisted her parents move to Madison so her father could have been treated at UW Hospital."

"It sounds as if the entire family wants to blame everything on Nancy and Sean," Rhonda observed. "I can't blame her for wanting to get away for a while. I think it's a good thing she's got somewhere to go where she can feel useful. The way I see it, she's been taking care of John and Beverly ever since Hank's death. It was a job none of Beverly's kids wanted to accept and Nancy was handy. I think Beverly appreciates everything Nancy has done for her, but she's outnumbered with the rest of her kids. It's a shame. I can't imagine being part of a family for so long and suddenly be told I'm no longer needed."

"Do you think they actually said such a thing to Nancy?" Phil asked.

"Not in so many words, but you know what they say about actions."

Rhonda pondered the circumstances surrounding Nancy where Hank's family was concerned. "I got so caught up in what Steve had to say, I didn't get to talk to Richard."

"I took the opportunity to talk to him," Sheriff Cantwell replied. "He's an interesting character, to say the very least. I don't know if I believe in all his mumbo jumbo about talking to the ancestors, but he certainly is spot on about the arrangement that was delivered to the funeral home, yesterday. He even knew about the note written on the inside of the envelope. It was so uncanny I asked if he would mind being fingerprinted before he leaves town tomorrow."

Rhonda was horrified. How could Sheriff Cantwell even consider Richard a suspect in this? He hadn't even been in the state when Sean was murdered.

"Don't look at me like that, Rhonda. In a circumstance like this, it's only natural. He certainly wasn't offended. As a matter of fact, that wily old fox was two steps ahead of me. He told me when he came in for his interview, he insisted on being fingerprinted. I checked before we left the church and found out we do have his prints on file."

"I'm willing to bet they don't match the ones they lifted from the arrangement," Phil said. "I'm as big a skeptic as the sheriff here when it comes to that psychic stuff, but somehow if that old man told me the sky was green, I'd believe him."

Rhonda smiled to herself. She remembered when Richard came in to be interviewed. At the time he said he and his wife enjoyed watching *Law & Order* on television. It didn't surprise her to learn he'd volunteered his fingerprint information so easily. Someone with nothing to hide would be more than happy to do anything to contradict any accusations that might be made against them. She secretly wished they would be able to ask everyone they interviewed to be fingerprinted.

Chapter Fourteen

As Rhonda predicted, Richard's fingerprints didn't match any of the ones lifted from the strange arrangement. She got the report after she'd conducted two more interviews of the girls who made up the homecoming court.

"How did your interviews go?" Phil asked, as they were getting ready to go home for the night.

"Better than the first ones I did. These girls had nothing but good things to say about Sean and were shocked and saddened by his murder. How about yours?"

"I'd have been happier if I could get in touch with Mike Yankton and his father. I've left numerous messages and they haven't returned any of my calls."

Rhonda knew of Phil's frustration. She'd felt it with both Crystal and Janice. "Let me talk to Mark tonight and find out if Mike has been at football practice this past week. If he's been ditching practice, I'll check to see if he's in his classes."

Once in her personal vehicle, Rhonda put on her seatbelt and contemplated the drive home. Today had been mentally and physically draining, to say the very least. To make matters worse, the snow that started falling when they left the cemetery continued all afternoon until now there were at least five inches of the early season snow on the ground.

"I've taken enough time on this pity party," she said aloud. "It's time to tackle the streets and get home." The fact she'd started talking to herself was of no concern, since she knew she was overly tired and needed to hear a familiar voice so she could face the drive home.

The highway in front of the sheriff's department was slushy because of the amount of traffic. She prayed the city streets would be equally free of snow, but knew as soon as she pulled off the main street everything would change.

Ahead of her, traffic slowed to a crawl and through the haze of swirling snow she saw flashing lights about a block beyond where her car was all but stopped. "Oh no, not an accident."

Her speedometer registered five miles an hour as she drove past the scene of the accident. A city officer stood in the rapidly falling snow directing traffic, allowing only one or two cars to enter the intersection from each direction at a time.

Rather than rubber neck at the wrecked cars blocking half of the intersection, she proceeded toward the turnoff for her subdivision.

She finally turned into her driveway, surprised to see the garage door opened and Mark scanning the street, waiting for her return.

"I was so worried," he said as soon as she pried her fingers from the steering wheel and got out of the vehicle. "I've been listening to the scanner and heard there was a bad accident on the corner of Alpine and Grand. I've been praying it wasn't you."

"I probably should have called you when I first saw it, but I was so intent on getting home, I didn't even think about using the hands free cell phone in the car."

"You're here now and that's all that matters," Mark said, he took her in his arms.

She enjoyed the security he offered. Here she wasn't Detective Pohs. Here she was Mark's wife and lover.

Once inside the kitchen, she glanced at the microwave clock and realized her fifteen-minute commute had taken her well over an hour. It was no wonder she felt so tired and stressed.

Almost immediately, the aroma of Mark's special chili made her mouth water. No matter what anyone said, she was blessed to have married a man who could cook. With her crazy schedule, if they had to wait for her to put a meal on the table, starvation might be a real option.

"You sit down and I'll dish up the chili," Mark said, holding out the chair for her.

Gratefully, Rhonda sat down and allowed the tension of the day to drain from her body. Mark had just put bowls of steaming chili on the table when her cell phone rang.

"Don't answer it," Mark suggested.

"Yeah, like that's going to happen. With an ongoing investigation, I can't ignore it."

"I know, but it's a good thought."

Rhonda picked up her phone, sticking her tongue out in Mark's direction at the same time. "Pohs here," she answered.

"I wanted to make sure you got home all right," Phil said.

"I finally got here, but something tells me my safety isn't what prompted this call."

"You're right. Did you happen to pass that bad accident on Alpine?"

The sight of the mangled vehicles blocking half of the intersection made Rhonda shudder. "I did, but I tried not to look too closely. I was having a hard enough time trying to get home and didn't need to stop and stare."

"I just got a call from Dan Yankton. He told me he was sick to death of my leaving messages. He also said he hoped we were happy because his son was in a bad accident and he was in the hospital."

The scene of the accident she'd passed on the way home again flashed in Rhonda's mind. "Are you saying he blames us?"

"You've got it. He believes we've harassed Mike so badly he wasn't paying attention and ran a red light, t-boning a car in the intersection. I checked with the city police and they're charging Mike with vehicular homicide along with DUI. His blood alcohol was one point four-five and the passenger in the other car, a thirty-five year old woman, was killed."

"But this is a school day. How could he be so drunk?"

"I asked the same thing, but school was out at three and the accident happened around five-fifteen. A kid can drink a lot of beer in two hours."

Rhonda nodded, knowing full well Phil couldn't see her gesture. "Should we go to the hospital?"

"There's no sense in us going out in this storm. From what Dan said, Mike's still in surgery. We won't be able to talk to him tonight and

Dan will probably try to keep us from getting access to his room."

Rhonda hung up the phone and looked into Mark's questioning eyes. "That accident I passed involved Mike Yankton, and he was drunk."

"It doesn't surprise me. I had to cut him from the football team this morning. I got a call from the principal's office about ten saying Mike was in his office and he was drunk. When I saw him, I had no option but to cut him. I have to say, the team is hurting with the loss of two star players."

"What about the bad blood between Sean and Mike? You talked about it in our interview the other day."

"Sean didn't have a problem with anyone. He was a good kid and didn't blame anyone, especially not Mike, for his prejudice. It amazed me how Mike's opinion of Sean changed when his Native American heritage became known. It never made sense to me. Of course, his drinking is nothing new."

"What do you mean?"

"I gave Mike a warning back in September when I found out he hosted a beer bash for the seniors out at his folks' farm. Everyone was there with the exception of Sean and Max. Since we only heard about it and didn't catch them in the act, the only thing we could do was issue a warning."

"Why didn't you tell me any of this before now?" Rhonda asked.

"Because it didn't have any bearing on your case. Mike's got a problem and I think a lot of it stems from his father. I have no doubt about who bought the beer for his little party. He's one of those guys who think it's all right to throw a party for his kids and serve alcohol as long as they keep the kids' keys. They think it makes them the kids' friends, especially when they don't get caught."

~ * ~

The snow continued throughout the night. It was five the next morning when Mark's phone started ringing. Rhonda turned over to face Mark, knowing such a call could only mean the storm hadn't completely passed and school was being called off.

"Snow day," he said as he burrowed down under the covers and pulled Rhonda into a loving embrace.

"For you maybe, but not for me. I have to get up and out of here to get ready for work. Do you know what that means?"

Mark kissed her before throwing back the covers. "It means I have to get up, brave the elements and clean out the driveway. To be truthful, I think I'll take you to work in my vehicle. I at least have four-wheel drive."

Rhonda took a moment to relax while Mark dressed in warm clothing before going out to run the snow blower. Once she heard the motor come to life, she got up and headed for the shower.

By the time Mark came in, Rhonda had breakfast on the table. The kitchen radio played in the background. "And now for our latest list of closings. We've checked and every school in the county is closed due to the unprecedented fourteen-inch snowfall overnight. The following companies are closed." Rhonda stopped listening. It didn't matter who closed what, the officers of the sheriff's department had to work.

Rhonda poured their coffee and sat down at the table as the local news came on the radio. "During last night's storm, there were numerous runoff accidents. There were two accidents, one in town and the other in the country resulting in fatalities. Thirty-five year old Sonja Thompson was killed when the car she was riding in was hit in the middle of the intersection of Alpine and Grand. Her husband, thirty-seven year old Ken, was taken to the hospital with non-life threatening injuries. The driver of the other car, eighteen-year old Michael Yankton, is in the hospital in critical condition. He is being charged with DUI and vehicular homicide. A one car, rollover accident on County O resulted in the death of forty-five year old Tamara Harrison. The storm is blamed for this fatality."

Rhonda switched off the reason. "There's a reason I don't like these early season snowstorms," she commented. "No one knows how to drive or if they do they've forgotten over the summer."

Before Mark could respond, Rhonda's phone began to ring. "Rhonda," Sheriff Cantwell greeted her. "You haven't left for work yet, have you?"

"No, we're just finishing breakfast. Since Mark's planning to drive me to the office, I didn't see any reason to hurry."

"I'm glad I caught you, then. Instead of going into the office, I want you to meet Phil at the hospital. He's going over there to see if he can interview Mike and Dan Yankton."

"Do you think we can get in to see him?"

"I checked with the hospital. He's listed in critical condition, but hopefully he can have visitors."

Sirens screamed all around them as they made their way toward the hospital. At least three times, they pulled over to allow emergency vehicles to pass on the partially plowed streets. Since the snow was still falling heavily, only the main arteries were being kept clean.

"Aren't you glad you didn't drive?" Mark asked once they pulled up in front of the entrance to the Emergency Room.

"You know I am. I just wish neither of us would have had to go out in this storm. I'll see if Phil can give me a lift home once we finish for the day." She leaned across the armrest of the vehicle and gave Mark a kiss before getting out to go into the hospital.

Phil waited for her in the reception area just inside the door. "Did you have any trouble getting in?" he questioned.

"Not really. Mark drove. His vehicle is like yours, a tank. How about you?"

"I got stuck getting out of my driveway, but it didn't take me long to rock the truck enough to get out."

Rhonda checked her watch. "It's nine. do you think the Yankton's will be here?"

"From what I found out, they never left the hospital last night. Mike didn't get out of surgery until after midnight. By that time, the storm was at its height. Since they remained at the hospital, they were put up in one of the family rooms next to ICU. I remember when my mom was up there, my sisters from out of town stayed there until the end finally came."

"Have you talked to them?"

"No. When I got here and checked in with the ICU department, I was told they were in with their son. He must be in pretty bad shape, since the nurse I talked to told me he can only have visitors for ten minutes out of every hour. My thought is to go to the cafeteria and see if we can find them there."

Rhonda agreed. Even though she hadn't driven to the hospital on her own, she needed a cup of coffee to calm her shattered nerves.

Being break time, nurses and doctors were among the patrons grabbing hot coffee and pastries for a mid-morning snack. Although not hungry, Rhonda looked forward to sitting and enjoying the comfort of a hot drink. She marveled at the large cinnamon roll Phil picked up, but said nothing. She decided he must have a high metabolism since he never seemed to gain weight. She, on the other hand, had to watch every morsel of food she ate so she didn't gain unwanted pounds.

Across the room, Rhonda spotted Dan and Anita Yankton sitting at a table close to the windows. She ached for the fatigue and worry she read in Anita's eyes.

"What the hell are you doing here?" Dan asked when Phil and Rhonda sat at the next table.

"For one thing," Rhonda replied, "we came to check on how Mike is doing."

"The hell you did. You came because you're feeling guilty about harassing our son so much he ended up here. I told your partner last night, this is all your fault."

"Dan! If anyone is to blame for what happened, it's you and Michael," Anita said, her voice edging between aggravation and exhaustion. Rhonda thought it sounded as though she were Dan's mother rather than his wife and was chastising him for some infraction.

"Me!"

Rhonda could feel a family fight erupting before her eyes.

"Yes, you. How many times did you tell Michael about the good old days when you were in school and the drinking age was eighteen? You were also the one who said drinking at home was all right. With both of us at work when he leaves for school, is it any wonder he started drinking more and more? What did it get him? I'll tell you what. He got suspended from school, kicked off the football team and is upstairs clinging to life by a thread. I hope you're happy now."

Sparks flashed between husband and wife. Rhonda was certain everything Anita just said had the ring of truth to it. There was no doubt Mike's drinking habit was something his father had instigated. She could see Dan handing his underage son a beer or maybe something stronger.

"You know all the calls this bastard has been making to Mike and me drove him to drink. I'm tempted to sue him and the entire sheriff's department for harassment."

"Listen to yourself, Dan," Anita pleaded. "One boy is dead and these people are trying to find out who was behind the murder. What if it had been Michael who was murdered? Wouldn't you want the authorities to go to any length to solve it?"

Dan seemed to lose some of his steam. "Why are you trying to get in touch with us, Detective? You can't believe either my son or I had anything to do with Sean's murder."

Rhonda wondered if the timing for this conversation was right. The Yanktons were under enough stress with their son in ICU in critical condition.

"We can go into that later," Phil said. "We really are interested in Mike's condition."

Anita burst into tears and Rhonda wished she could comfort the older woman. It wasn't as though they were friends. She was the detective investigating a murder and this woman's son and husband were persons of interest she wanted to interview. In no way could she let her guard down even with the dire circumstances these people faced.

Dan took a deep breath. "There was a bad head injury. They fixed what they could in surgery, but it's left him in a coma. If he survives this, he probably won't ever be the same. It's possible he'll be legally blind and mentally handicapped. It would have been better if he'd died on impact."

"Please don't say that," Anita sobbed. "I don't care what shape he's in. He's my son. I'll take care of him for the rest of his life rather than have to visit him at the cemetery the way Nancy Richardson has to do with her son."

Rhonda remembered a childhood friend who had been in a

horrific accident when he was sixteen. He'd been out with friends and was a passenger in the front seat. As she recalled, he'd been comatose for three months and left legally blind and would never have a mental age of more than six years. Although the lifetime commitment had been all consuming, she knew the boy's mother was more than willing to do whatever it took to have her son in her life. If anyone were to ask her today, it was certain she would say whatever she had to do was worth any sacrifice.

Anger again filled Dan's eyes. "You're saying my son had something to do with that half-breed's murder, aren't you?"

"On the contrary, Mr. Yankton," Rhonda replied, trying to remain as calm as she could. "We're talking to every member of the football team, including my husband. We're also talking to the cheerleaders and the female members of the homecoming court. It's no secret Mike and his friend Adam tried to have Sean replaced as captain of the football team. It's also no secret you and Adam's father were in favor of their actions because of Sean's heritage."

"That's right, dammit. Why should some dirty Indian take a place on the football team that should have belonged to my son who is white? Why wasn't he on the reservation where he belonged?"

Rhonda's anger threatened to boil over. In this day and age, such bigoted behavior was completely uncalled for.

"I understand you need to find Sean's murderer," Anita said. "I never understood Dan's warped feelings. Until Sean returned from South Dakota last August, he was always welcome in our family. I've known or suspected Nancy had some Indian heritage. I've never mentioned it because of Dan's reaction to that Native American mascot fiasco. Until that happened, I never knew how he felt."

Before Anita could continue, her cell phone rang. After glancing at the caller ID, she held the phone out to Dan.

"Hello," he answered. "Yes, yes, we'll be right up."

Dan and Anita both pushed back their chairs. "You'll have to excuse us," Dan said, his voice laced with concern for his son. "As far as I'm concerned, this meeting was uncalled for and is definitely over. That was the nurse from ICU. The doctor wants to see us."

Phil nodded. The seriousness of the look on Dan and Anita's faces told Rhonda the news from ICU could not be good.

"Do you still think either Mike or Dan could be involved in Sean's murder?" Rhonda asked once they were alone.

"I don't think so. They're both bigots, that's for sure, but people like them rarely do more than talk. If push comes to shove, I doubt either of them would ever take a physical stand. I think our best bet is to concentrate on the sender of the e-mail as well as that of the arrangement."

Rhonda took a drink of her now-cold coffee and glanced out the window. Rather than diminishing, the snow continued to fall, making her wonder how they would be able to get back to the office.

In the parking lot, she was surprised to see Phil's snow-covered vehicle. It was evident he hadn't taken an official vehicle. For that, she was pleased. A car could easily get stuck in the drifting snow as it continued to pile up to an unheard-of amount for so early in the season. Hopefully, Phil's SUV would get them back to the office safely.

Being a gentleman, Phil offered to go out to his truck and bring it up for her to get in. As good as his suggestion sounded, she opted to go out to the truck with him. There were at least two or three additional inches of snow on the windows as well as the body of the truck. It would take the two of them quite some time to get it all cleaned off.

Phil walked ahead of her, not paying attention to the snow-covered parking lot. While she slowly picked her way along, she watched as Phil slipped on a patch of ice. Even though it wasn't proper, she laughed at him falling into a drift.

"It's not funny, Rhonda," Phil said when she offered him her hand in assistance in getting up.

"It was from where I was standing. Are you hurt?"

"Only my pride. I'll get the truck started when I pull out the snowbrushes. Just because you laughed at me, I should make you clean off all this snow alone while I nurse my ego."

"It wouldn't bother me. Of course, any help you'd like to offer would be appreciated, that is if your bruised ego will allow it."

Phil used his remote to unlock the truck and then proceeded to clean the snow off the driver's door. As he did, he made a snowball and threw it in Rhonda's direction. Being so early in the season, the snow didn't pack well and the snowball fell apart before it could do more than shower her with the cold flakes.

It took about ten minutes to finish cleaning the snow from the windows and hood of the truck. From Phil's drive to the hospital, the warm windows had become covered with ice as the new snow fell on them. By the time they finished, the interior of the cab was warm and inviting.

"Before we head back, we should check in with the office," Phil suggested. "If we're lucky, they won't want us to come back. There's not much we can do in this storm."

"Like that's going to happen in our lifetime. This is little more than another day at work. You know we can always make phone calls and look over the evidence we have on this case. Maybe we're barking up the wrong tree with our ideas about the football team and cheerleaders."

"Maybe we are, but I still have a funny feeling about Mike and Adam."

~ * ~

Rhonda and Phil went back to the office and had been there for almost three hours before the storm finally abated. Together they went over the recordings of the interviews they'd conducted in the case until Rhonda's phone rang.

"Rhonda," a very unsteady female voice greeted her. "This is Anita Yankton. I wanted to keep you informed about Michael. The call we got was to have us come up to ICU because he suffered a stroke. They've put him on life support. I don't know..."

"Oh, Anita, I am so sorry. Is there anything we can do to help you?"

"Yes, please pray. At this point, we won't know what will happen for forty-eight hours. I also wanted to apologize for Dan's outburst this morning. We're both exhausted. I know that's not an excuse because with all my heart I know Dan is responsible for Michael's attitude as well as his drinking. I threatened to leave when he was making such a fuss about the mascot. If I'd realized how far it was going to go, I should have followed through. At least then Michael wouldn't have been under his father's control." By the time the call ended, Rhonda was shaking.

"What's wrong?" Phil asked.

Rhonda wished she'd put the phone on speaker when she first answered it. That way she wouldn't have to repeat the devastating news Anita just told her. Instead she told Phil everything Anita had said. "I just don't know how much Mark cutting Mike from the football team had to do with yesterday's drinking," she concluded.

"Probably quite a bit, although didn't you say he was cut and suspended from school because he was drunk when he got there yesterday morning? If that's the case, Mark's involvement wasn't the biggest contributing factor in last night's accident."

"Do you think we should call Mark and see just how drunk Mike was yesterday morning when he was in the principal's office?"

Before Phil could answer, Rhonda's phone rang again. When she saw Nancy Richardson's number on the caller ID, she put the phone on speaker before picking it up.

"I just heard about the Yankton boy," Nancy said, initiating the conversation. "I don't like to intrude at a time like this, but Grandfather told me there was a reason why the snow came and we couldn't leave for South Dakota today. I hope I can be of comfort to Anita. I've always considered her as a friend. Have you talked to her?"

Rhonda blessed Nancy's heart of gold but wondered about the prudence of her making contact with the Yankton family. Even though Anita might be receptive, she wondered about Dan's reaction to any contact from Nancy.

"I'm certain they're spending most of their time at the hospital. You know how things were when Hank was so sick." She hoped Nancy would understand what she was trying to say.

"Of course, since we rescheduled our flight for tomorrow, I'll just send a card to the house with my cell phone number. The real reason for my call is that Grandfather has had more communication with regard to

Sean's service. He wanted to tell you not to be confused by the arrangement sent to the funeral home for John's funeral. It was not sent by anyone involved in Sean's murder. It was nothing more than a cruel joke."

Rhonda exchanged a questioning glance with Phil. "Thank you, I think," she replied, not at all sure she should take this new information concerning the case as gospel.

"I know Grandfather's visions are confusing. They are for me, and I can only imagine how they sound to you. I had very little contact with my grandparents while I was growing up. Although my mother loved her parents, Minneapolis seemed like a million miles away from South Dakota back then. She made the choice to marry into the white world and forsake her heritage. I'm so glad Sean had his time in South Dakota last summer. I'm also looking forward to having my own experience now. Grandfather said he would stay in touch with you and let you know anything the spirits impart to him."

Phil's raised eyebrows told Rhonda he too questioned Richard's visions, but at this point they were willing to grab at any straws they could get. Without saying a word, Phil left the office, leaving Rhonda to continue her conversation with Nancy.

They talked for several more minutes before ending the call. Yesterday Rhonda would have believed anything Richard told her. With the events of the past twenty-four hours, she didn't know what to believe. On Sunday, Richard said all was not as it seemed, leading her away from the football team and cheerleaders. At the visitation, the strange arrangement seemed as though it had come from the murderer. Now she didn't know which way to turn.

"It's time to call it a day," Phil said when he returned to her office, carrying her coat in his hand. "I'll give you a lift home. I called the wife and told her I wanted some soup for supper. I swear I'm chilled completely to the bone."

Rhonda smiled. She thought about last night when Mark's chili had been exactly what she needed to warm her body. If she were lucky, maybe there would be some left over for her to savor tonight.

Mark was just finishing clearing the driveway and sidewalk when

Phil pulled in. "You're just a little too late," Mark quipped. "I could have used some help with this now. I hear the final inch count was twenty-four."

Rhonda looked at the huge piles of blown snow on either side of the driveway. She had no doubt about what Mark said concerning the snowfall.

"If you didn't look so whipped, I'd ask you to come over and help me with my snow. Of course I've got teenagers, but you know how kids are. I'm sure they left the lion's share of the work for the old man."

"I hear you there. When I was a kid and had a snow day, my mom had to actually threaten me to get me to go out and shovel the snow. I guess I finally grew out of that stage in my life. If I hadn't, Rhonda would be out there with me until late into the night."

"Ah, I guess that means I'm going to have to do the cooking tonight," Rhonda teased.

"Oh, my dear wife, you do underestimate me. I got a new recipe from one of the teachers at school. It's called dump soup. I put it in the crock pot this morning. It should be ready by the time we get into the house."

"If I'm lucky, my supper will be ready when I get home. I'll need some fortification to face that driveway and sidewalk. I'll see you in the morning, Rhonda."

They watched as Phil pulled out of the driveway as though maneuvering his vehicle through a snow canyon.

"I can't believe you got this all done by yourself," Rhonda said, as they went into the house.

"Don't tell Phil, but Jim Fenton came by with his new toy. He got a plow for his lawn tractor and did the driveway for me. All I had left to use the snow blower on were the sidewalks and they didn't take much time."

Inside their cozy kitchen, Rhonda noticed the large soup bowls along with a loaf of bread. She knew it was a frozen loaf, but the thought of it made her mouth water. After changing from her heavy coat, boots and business suit, she finally made it to the table wearing sweats and slipper socks.

"That's much better," she said as she sat down at her place at the table.

"I know what you mean." Rhonda took a moment to check out her husband's attire. Outside he'd been wearing a snowmobiling suit, stocking cap, boots and heavy mittens. Now he looked just as comfortable as she felt in his black sweat pants and his sweatshirt with the logo for the high school on it.

"How is Mike?" Mark asked, once he ladled the soup into their bowls.

Rhonda tasted her soup and then took a deep breath before answering. "We talked to Dan and Anita Yankton this morning. There were terrible head injuries involved. Do you remember my friend Randy?"

Mark nodded. "We hadn't moved here yet when the accident happened, but I heard the guys at school talking about it."

"Well, that's the shape Mike is in now. We were still talking when they received a call from ICU. By the time we got back to the office, Anita called me and said Mike suffered a stroke. He's on life support. I'm afraid it's only a matter of time."

"I just don't understand how parents allow their teenage kids to drink like that."

"Get real, Mark. Don't you remember what it was like to be a teenager? Sneaking a beer behind your parents' backs was almost the national pastime way back when. The problem with Mike is that Dan approved of his drinking. I don't think he had any idea of how much his son was drinking. It's real easy for kids to drink when both of their parents leave for work before they go to school. I'm sure Mike thought he could get by with a drink in the morning, especially since he was drinking vodka in his orange juice. Kids don't think vodka can be smelled on their breath."

Mark wrinkled his nose as though remembering the smell of the alcohol on Mike's breath the day before when he came to school drunk. "I guess you're right. At that age it didn't matter what we did, we all thought we were indestructible. I don't ever remember driving drunk, but I'm sure I did it at one time or another. It was that 'nothing can happen to me' attitude that does all the kids in. In this case, not only did Mike's actions cause the death of another person, it quite possibly cost him his life."

Rhonda nodded. She didn't think this case was ever going to come to an end. Until last night her best suspect had been Mike and his bigoted attitude toward Sean. Now she wasn't so sure.

"It probably would be a good thing for you to contact the school and set up another counseling session for the kids tomorrow."

"I'm way ahead of you. Considering the severity of the accident, I thought it would be best if we talked to the kids. I'm sure there will be rumors about Mike being cut from the football team and being suspended from school. Like I said, these kids think nothing bad can ever happen to them and that drinking is way cool. I talked with several of the other teachers this morning and they all agree with me. From the weather report, they're expecting high winds tonight, so there may not be any school, but we're prepared to have an all school assembly on what has happened, if we aren't closed. I was supposed to ask you if you would be willing to come to talk to the kids."

"You know I will," Rhonda replied. It seemed quite amazing that in all the years she and Mark had been married, she'd never had cause to go to the school where he worked for anything other than to watch the football games. Now because of the things that had happened in the past few weeks, she would be going there for the third time, to say nothing of dealing with more teenagers than ever before.

Chapter Fifteen

The wind the weatherman predicted picked up overnight and lasted throughout the rest of the week. School did not reopen until Monday. Rhonda heard from Nancy Richardson on a regular basis since the flights out of Madison were also grounded. The entire area was in the grip of a full-blown winter storm. Not only were the winds strong, but also more snow came to add to the chaos. The weatherman constantly said the storm was going to move on, but it seemed to be stuck over the entire area as well as the rest of the Midwest.

Sunday afternoon, Rhonda received word Mike Yankton had been taken off life support and passed away. She knew Mike's death would be a blow to the entire community.

On Monday morning, Rhonda and Phil arrived at the high school just prior to nine. Mark waited to escort them to the auditorium. Coming in from the back of the stage area, they could hear the murmurs of the students sitting in the plush seats of the main floor as well as the balcony.

Along with Rhonda and Phil were several of the teachers, the principal and the same counselors who had come to the school after Sean's murder.

"Good morning," the principal greeted the students after the initial screech of the sound system being activated. "I am certain you have all heard the rumors. We are here to give you the facts and to let you know exactly what happened. I now turn the floor over to Coach Pohs."

Mark got to his feet and stepped up to the microphone. "Three weeks ago today, we were here to counsel you about the murder of Sean Richardson. Today we are here because of another student. Last Wednesday morning, Michael Yankton arrived at school drunk. I was called into the principal's office, and yes, he was cut from the football team and suspended from school. I know a lot of you believe drinking is your God-given right and you think you are grown up enough to be able to drink if you want to. I am here today to tell you there is nothing further from the truth."

Rhonda listened to the gasps from the assembly. Either not all of the students had heard about the suspension or they didn't believe it.

"As your teachers and coaches, we want you to know underage drinking will not be tolerated in this school. Unfortunately, Mike didn't believe we could have any control over him. He spent the rest of the day drinking and took off in his car in the midst of the primary snowstorm that hit the area. The result of his actions was his running a stoplight and killing a woman in another car. Mike suffered some severe head injuries and yesterday afternoon his parents made the most agonizing decision a parent ever has to make. They decided to take him off life support. He passed away only minutes later."

Girls in the auditorium screamed and sobbed loudly, causing Mark to pause until they quieted down enough to listen to what he said.

"We are here today to answer any questions you might have as well as to stress to you the importance of respecting your bodies enough not to drink until you are adults and if you do, not to drive."

Rhonda noticed a commotion at the back of the room and looked up to see several adults coming down the side aisles. As they got closer, she recognized many of the parents of the members of the football team and cheerleading squad coming toward the stage. They came up to stand in front of the teachers and counselors who sat at the back.

"We've come here today because Coach Pohs called us last night and told us why they were having this assembly," Allan Cleary said into the microphone. "Sean's death was a horrific murder and we've all been trying to come to grips with it. Now Mike has been taken from us as well. His was not a death brought about because of a drive-by shooting, but driving was involved. Yes, it was an accident, but it was an accident caused by a bottle of vodka. You will all mourn his passing and your parents will breathe a sigh of relief to know they aren't the ones having to make funeral arrangements. We're here to tell you only you can keep it that way. If you knew and liked Mike, we urge you to think twice before you decide to try drinking even as much as a beer. Please think before you act."

Several more parents voiced the same opinion. Finally Mark took the microphone. "We've decided Sean and Mike should be remembered, so we wanted to write up a contract between the kids and the parents saying we won't permit underage drinking and you will not drink until you are of legal age. Once this agreement is signed, each parent will donate what they can to a scholarship in Sean and Michael's name. The parents of the football team and cheerleading squad are sponsoring their kids in the amount of one hundred dollars per family. We realize all parents can't afford this much, but we will take any donation you can give. We want to keep all of our children sober and give them a chance to receive the scholarship."

"Am I too late?" A woman's voice sounded from the back of the room. Rhonda strained to see who it was. When Nancy Richardson stepped onto the stage, Rhonda could hardly believe her eyes.

"I've been told about this scholarship. It's too late for me to have my son sign the pledge, but I do think there is something I can do. At Sean's funeral, we received memorial money. I cannot think of any better way to spend it. I have a check for five thousand dollars to put into the fund. When Grandfather and I return to South Dakota, we will be telling the story of Sean and Michael's death to the people and starting similar programs for the people there. I know Sean thought of all of you as his friends. His spirit has been in contact with Grandfather's spirit. He's pleased the money will be spent for education. He also told Grandfather his spirit met Mike and now they both walk with the ancestors."

"You speak of the ancestors as though they are real," someone called from the assembly. "Are they ghosts?"

Nancy smiled at the question. "The Sioux believe they are spirits. They do not haunt the people. They guide them, using the wisdom of the ages."

"Do the spirits speak to everyone?"

"The Sioux are very spiritual, but not everyone can converse with the ancients. This is the job of the shaman. He is the one who has been given the gift of communication with the ancients. My grandfather has this gift and when Sean visited him last summer, his gift was revealed."

Nancy answered question after question. Rhonda realized if Sean's classmates had been given this information at the beginning of the school year, things might have been different. If nothing else, this was Nancy's parting gift to Sean's friends as well as the community.

With the assembly ended. Rhonda prepared to do individual counseling sessions in the gym when Nancy stopped her.

"I just had a call from Grandfather. We're leaving for the airport in Madison in two hours. We've been delayed for too long by this storm. Please keep in touch with us."

Rhonda hugged Nancy and promised to let her know of any news regarding the investigation. She watched as Nancy left through the front doors. Seeing Sean's mother leave his school for the last time made Rhonda wonder if she would be able to crack this case and bring Sean's murderer to justice.

One after another, the students she'd seen weeks ago after Sean's murder stopped to talk to her. Many of the athletes knew her as Mark's wife and with that connection, she was able to use his office as her station.

"Is it true about Mike getting cut from the team for drinking?" Adam Brinks asked. "Are you sure it wasn't because of that silly scarecrow we made up for Sean's grandpa's funeral?"

Rhonda's attention immediately focused on Adam.

"What do you know about the scarecrow?"

"Should my dad be with me? We didn't do anything wrong."

Mark stepped over to where Rhonda sat talking to Adam. "If you want your dad here with you, I'll go and see if he's still here." Before leaving the room, he motioned for Rhonda to follow him. "I'll get Phil to come with me. I'll also see if I can find a tape recorder."

Rhonda silently thanked Mark for his insight. Even though Adam was eighteen, she knew she should withhold any further questions until Steve Brinks could be found and brought into the office. She also knew it was best if Phil was with her to witness any information that might come to light. Like Mike and Dan, Adam and Steve had continually avoided coming into the office to be interviewed. With the bigoted opinions Dan expressed complimenting Steve's outlook on life, she could understand why they didn't think her investigation of Sean's murder was important enough to respect the reason they wanted to talk to both him and his son.

"What the hell is going on now?" Rhonda heard Steve say, even though the office door was closed. "First the cops are harassing Mike Yankton and my son and now you're dragging me down here to your office. Are you planning to cut my son from the football team just because he's not thrilled with playing ball with a half-breed?"

Rhonda opened the door to the office, "Look, Mr. Brinks," Mark began as they approached the area where she stood waiting for them "I didn't have any intention of cutting Adam from the football team when he first came in for counseling. The reason Mike was cut was because he came to school drunk. No matter what you think, it didn't have anything to do with Sean Richardson."

"Drunk? Are you out of your mind? He wouldn't have been drinking the night of the accident if it hadn't been for you. I hope you're happy knowing his death and that of the woman in the other car rests squarely on your shoulders."

"I think you have the facts wrong, Steve," Phil said from behind them. "Mike had been drinking for a long time. It was confirmed he came to school drunk on Wednesday. When we talked to Dan and Anita at the hospital, they confirmed that Mike had a drinking problem for the last several months. He just never allowed it to hinder his performance at school or on the football team. It was his father's warped ideas that led him to..."

Rhonda listened as Phil's words trailed off. Steve pushed past her to enter the room.

"Have they hurt you, son? Who in their right mind left you alone with this woman cop? She's..."

"I'm what, Steve? You've known me for years. To begin with, your son isn't a minor. We asked you to come here as a courtesy."

"And you brought in your partner. What's that all about?"

"Why don't you take a seat, and I'll tell you. Before we start, I have to ask you to leave the room, Mark. This is a police investigation."

The questions in her husband's eyes would have to wait. There was no way she wanted to involve him in this until all the facts came to light and all the cards were on the table.

She waited until Mark left the room and Steve pulled a chair up to the desk beside where Adam sat. "On Tuesday night I went to the funeral home for John Richardson. When the funeral director arrived, there was an arrangement sitting outside the front door. Until now, the only people who knew about it were the personnel at the funeral home, the sheriff's office and Richard Brave Beaver, Sean's great-grandfather." The look on Steve's face was one of complete shock.

"What does that have to do with anything?"

"Did you know about it?" Phil asked.

"Know about it? I helped the kids buy the stuff and delivered it in my truck. It was a tribute to John from the boys. They knew they wouldn't be welcome at the visitation and if they sent something, the family wouldn't accept it. We thought it was best if they did something anonymously. What's wrong with that?"

"Who wrote the message on the condolence card?"

"What are you getting at? I thought the arrangement was very tasteful."

Rhonda shook her head. "Do you have any idea what the condolence card even said?"

"I do," Adam said, speaking for the first time. "Mike wrote it and it said, Rest in Peace Mr. Richardson. Thanks for the Memories."

Rhonda turned her attention to Adam. "Are you sure that's what he wrote? Did you know what was written on the inside of the envelope?"

"Of course I am. I saw him write it. As for the inside, why would anything be written there?"

"The message you're telling me about isn't the same as the one on the arrangement at the time it was delivered. On the inside of the envelope, there was another message. It read: it's so much fun to watch you squirm—catch me if you can, Detective Pohs. Did you have any idea why Mike would write such a thing?"

Adam hung his head. "I don't know what you're talking about. I just know that after my dad delivered the arrangement, Mike said he was going back to rearrange it. I told him I didn't want any part in it. I just wanted Mr. Richardson to know that someone remembered what he did on Halloween and..."

"And what?" Phil asked, when Adam paused.

"Mike took me out to the quarry, and he had another Jacko-lantern in his car. He took out a pistol. I think it was one his dad has for target shooting. After he put the Jacko-lantern up on one of the rocks, he stepped back and took aim at it. I was shocked when he put a hole in the head right where the papers say Sean was shot. He said he was going to take it to the funeral home and replace the one we put on the arrangement. I told him he was out of his mind and that was just plain mean. I didn't like Sean after what we learned about him being part Indian, but I didn't want him dead and I didn't think something like that was right to send to his family."

"Are you sure about all of this?" Steve asked.

"Like I said, Dad, it was a joke. Since the pumpkin head Sean was wearing was shot through, Mike said it was only proper. I didn't go with Mike, but he said it was best for you to leave it off intact and then exchange it for the doctored up one later."

"Where is the original one, Adam?" Phil asked.

"I don't know. I didn't see Mike after I went home. I was scared when he took out that gun. He also had a flask of vodka and wanted me to drink with him. I told him no way. I didn't want any part of his drinking. He told me I was a wuss and after he shot the hole in the jack-o-lantern, he dropped me off downtown and took off toward the funeral home."

"I have to ask," Rhonda continued, "did you and Mike have anything to do with Sean's murder?"

"I—I..."

"Answer the lady, Adam!" Steve shouted, pulling Adam to his feet by his shirt collar.

"Take your hands off your son," Phil ordered. "Now, Adam, we'll ask you again. Did you have anything to do with the murder of Sean Richardson?"

"No, sir. Mike said he wished he'd thought of it. He said as a half-breed we didn't want Sean around here, but I told him that was dumb. He was just talking out of his ass. We both knew he wouldn't have had the balls to do anything about it. He figured the cops would suspect him because once Sean was dead, he was going to be captain of the football team just like he should have been all along."

"Would you take a polygraph test, Adam?" Rhonda asked.

"A what?" Adam inquired

"A lie detector test, you idiot," Steve roared. "My son just told you he had nothing to do with that murder. Why don't you believe him?"

"Calm down," Phil said, putting his hand on Steve's shoulder. "We're just doing our job."

Rhonda took a deep breath before repeating her previous question. "Are you willing to take a polygraph test, Adam?"

"Yes, ma'am. I want you to know I didn't have anything to do with killing Sean. Until Mike said he was nothing but a dirty Indian, I liked him, I really did. I wouldn't kill him."

"But you knew about the switched out pumpkin head, didn't you?"

"Like I said, I told him I didn't want anything to do with it. He said he didn't want me along anyway."

"Why weren't you at football practice?" Steve asked.

"We didn't practice on Tuesday, because Coach Pohs said he wanted to go to the visitation for John Richardson and I told the boys they had the night off."

"You told me you had practice so you couldn't help deliver that thing to the funeral home," Steve accused.

"That's because Mike said it was best if we weren't seen dropping it off. Instead we went to the quarry. Mike said we had plenty of time to sneak back in after you left. I knew it wouldn't be hard with that new funeral home so far out in the country. Mike said there wouldn't be anyone around and..."

"Shut up, you fool," Steve said giving his son a look that shot daggers. "You aren't going to say another word until we get you a lawyer."

"Am I under arrest?" Adam asked.

"No, Adam, you aren't under arrest," Rhonda assured him. "I would appreciate it if you would come out to the sheriff's office for that polygraph test. Once your father gets you a lawyer, you can call my office and set up an appointment." She handed him one of her business cards and watched as Adam and Steve left Mark's office.

"How did everything go?" Mark asked when he came back into the office after Steve and Adam left.

Rhonda smiled at her husband. "Better than I expected."

~ * ~

After talking to several more members of the football team, Rhonda and Phil finally left the school. On the way back to the office, they stopped for something to eat.

"What do you make about the things the Brinks' kid told us?" Phil asked, once they were seated in a secluded booth.

"I honestly don't think he had anything to do with either the murder or switching out the jack-o-lantern. He's a follower and I think what he saw Mike do out at that quarry scared him shitless. I think we should contact the office and have them search Mike's car. I'm almost positive we'll find the original jack-o-lantern in there. As for the condolence card, I don't know how much of what Adam said about that I can believe. I think he knew exactly what it said. The thing that bothers me is that Steve didn't look at the card the kids put in the scarecrow's hand."

Chapter Sixteen

By the time Rhonda returned to her office, Mike's car had been searched and the intact jack-o-lantern found in the trunk where Adam said it would be.

"Are you going to tell the Yanktons about what we found?" Phil asked, as he stared at the fiberglass pumpkin in the evidence property room.

"I don't think the timing is right. They have a funeral to plan and live through, plus the nightmare of the lawsuit that will be filed by the other driver. They lost their son, but he lost his wife and will want compensation.

"What about Adam? Are we going to be able to charge him?"

Rhonda gave Phil's question a moment of thought. "I still want him to take the polygraph test. I've got a call in to the district attorney as to what charges can be filed. In my opinion, I'd say he's guilty of malicious mischief. Then there's Steve's participation in all of this. I don't know if he's guilty of anything, but he helped the boys buy and build the arrangement and he delivered it, even though there wasn't anything offensive about it at the time. The smashed pumpkin head was added later."

"What do you think about the note? It was directed at you."

"That's a matter of opinion. Before I answer that, I want to check out Mike's car for myself. I'm willing to bet we'll find another condolence card there. I also want to talk to Mark."

"Why?"

"Because something tells me there was more going on than just Mike's drinking." Rhonda pulled out her cell phone and placed a call to Mark.

"Hi honey," he greeted her. "I know you love me, but you just left my office. Do you miss me that much?"

"You're funny. I need you to stop by my office on your way home. I have some more questions about the case and I want to get your response on tape."

"Should I be worried?"

"What do you think? I'll see you around four."

Rhonda closed her phone, then turned to face Phil. "Let's go down to the impound lot and see what we can find."

"They've already got the jack-o-lantern, Rhonda. Are you sure you want to go out in the cold to look for something that might not exist?"

"You bet I do."

Phil shook his head and took their coats from the rack before holding Rhonda's so she could put it on. "Lead on, MacDuff. As much as I don't want to go back out in this weather, I do tend to agree with you on this one."

At the impound lot, Rhonda showed her badge and asked where to find Mike's car. As soon as she saw it, she marveled that Mike was able to survive as long as he did. The front end of the vehicle was completely smashed in.

"What are you looking for, Detective Pohs?" The lot attendant asked.

"A small white envelope with a condolence card in it," Rhonda replied. "I think it might be in the trunk."

The attendant shook his head. "We didn't see anything like that. You're welcome to go through everything, though."

"Have you checked out the interior?"

"We were told to check out the contents of the trunk. I don't even know if you can get into the interior. It's pretty beat up, you know, no room to even move around."

"Do you mind if we check it out?"

"Of course not. If you can get to it, you might find something in the glove box."

Rhonda agreed and pulled her coat closer around her neck to ward off the cold. In the cramped passenger compartment, Rhonda pried open the glove box and with plastic gloves removed the contents and put them into an evidence bag. It was too cold to go through everything, so she took it back into the office where she could put it out onto one of the tables.

"It's certainly warmer in here," Phil commented as Rhonda started to inventory the contents of the glove box.

"This all looks like the kind of stuff I'd expect to find," she said, as she went through the packet containing the owner's manual. "Nothing unusual here."

"Maybe you haven't found anything," Phil commented, "but I think I hit the mother lode."

Rhonda turned to see what had Phil so excited. When she did, she focused on the box containing the contents of Mike's trunk.

"This kid must have thought he was God's great gift to women. There are three unopened boxes of condoms, as well as two that are opened. At least he was interested in variety; they're all the expensive ribbed kind. Along with that I found a fifth of vodka."

Phil's mention of vodka brought to mind Adam's remark about Mike drinking at the quarry and how he said he didn't want any part of it. "That must be his main stash," she commented. "I found a flask of the stuff in his glove box." Phil held up one of the opened boxes of condoms and opened it. "Well, well, well, what is this?" he said pulling a small white envelope from the folded foil packs containing the condoms. "I think this is what we're looking for."

Rhonda carefully took the envelope from Phil and pulled out the card. In the same neat printing she remembered from the other card, she saw the original note. Rest in Peace Mr. Richardson. Thanks for the Memories. Instead of the message in red ink, the interior of the envelope was blank.

"Great job. We'll turn all this over to the forensics team." She glanced at her watch. We'd better get back up to the office. Mark should be there soon."

After the bite of the November air, Rhonda was glad to be back in her office. Even the property room was cooler than she liked.

Mark arrived shortly after four. "I've wracked my brain all

afternoon, but I have no idea what more I can tell you."

Rhonda waited until they were in one of the interrogation rooms with the tape recorder catching Mark's every word before she asked the questions that had come to mind since leaving the school earlier in the day.

"What has been going on with the football team since Sean's death?"

"I don't see what you're getting at," Mark replied. From the look in his eyes, Rhonda knew he was completely baffled by her question.

"I asked you to leave the room when we talked to Adam and Steve this morning. You did hear us mention the arrangement, but I'm sure you had no idea what we were talking about." She continued to tell Mark about the strange arrangement the funeral director found when he opened for the visitation on Tuesday night and didn't leave out the shattered jack-o-lantern used as the head.

"Do you think the kids were behind that?"

"I know they were. When we searched Mike's car, we found some very interesting things including the original jack-o-lantern. There were also two condolence notes."

"Two?" Mark questioned.

"The one we found with the arrangement said Rest in Peace Pumpkin Head. On the inside of the envelope was a note to me saying, *It's so much fun to watch you squirm-Catch me if you can, Detective Pohs.* The note was addressed to me, but somehow I'm getting the impression it was meant for you."

The look of shock on Mark's face turned to one of complete understanding. "It was such a minor thing; I dismissed it almost as soon as it happened. Right after Sean's funeral, Mike and Adam came to me and suggested Mike should be made captain of the football team. I listened to what they had to say and then called a meeting of the entire team. We put it to a vote. Needless to say, the team voted it down. They said Sean was our captain and they wanted to dedicate the remainder of the season to him. Of course the way things are going we may not be playing our game this week and who knows if we'll be able to even complete the schedule. With both Sean and Mike gone from the team, our offense has been compromised. I don't know if we can successfully compete."

"When did the team know they wouldn't have practice on Tuesday?"

"I told them when we practiced on Monday. I knew when the visitation would be and I thought I might not be the only one who wanted to pay my respects to the family. Sean was a member of our team and quite often John and Beverly would host parties for the team at their place. Everybody thought of them as surrogate grandparents."

"That answers a lot of questions. The thing I want to know now is if you think either Mike or Adam could have been capable of murdering Sean."

Mark shook his head. Rhonda had seen him locked in such mental conflict as he contemplated more and more of the possible answers formulating in his mind. "I honestly don't think so. Mike was a hothead and spouted off his mouth without thinking. I thought it was so sad, since he and Sean were good friends before last summer. I thought it had something to do with Mike dating Crystal. From the locker room talk, I don't think Sean and Crystal were having sexual relations, but it was different with Mike. He's always bragging about his conquests in the bedroom. I finally sat down with the entire team and talked to them about the dangers of having unprotected sex."

Mark's comment broke the tension in the room for the first time. "I think Mike took you seriously. We found several boxes of condoms in his car. I guess I didn't realize just how much access these kids have to things like that. When people have the kind of money the Yanktons have, maybe they bought them for him. At least they bought the best and most up to date ones. Maybe I should write down the names of them and we could give them a try."

Mark laughed. "Are you telling me you want to be more adventurous?"

"It could be, but not until I figure out this case. It really has me baffled."

"I know what you mean. I thought I knew these kids better than anyone, but I certainly missed Mike's drinking problem and the volcano that was brewing just beneath the surface over Sean's heritage. I heard all about his experiences last summer and realized it had affected him more than any of us understood. Maybe I should have expected some resentment considering all the flak in this town over the high school mascot, even though it was several years ago. I didn't think the sentiments ran quite so deep on the issue before this."

"Do you agree with me about the note?"

"I think I do. Mike wasn't happy when I told him we were going to put his idea about becoming the captain of the football team to a vote. He thought I'd just say he was the logical choice and that would be that."

Rhonda nodded. The note finally made sense. It wasn't an admission of guilt; it was aimed at Mark and the decision to put the position of captain of the football team to a vote of the other players. Sean had been a well-liked young man and even though Mike was a member of the same team, he never held the respect of his teammates.

By the time Rhonda finished questioning her husband, it was time for her to call it a day. Like most of the days since Sean's murder, she was more than ready to go home and relax away from the drama of the investigation.

Mark made it home before Rhonda and had the table set as soon as she walked in the door. He'd also brought in the evening paper. It came as no surprise to see the headlines stating the young man responsible for the fatal accident of less than a week earlier had died of his injuries.

On the obituary page, the graduation picture of Mike Yankton accompanied an obituary listing his achievements in school as well as his glory on the football field. Of course, there was no mention of the drinking that caused his death, nor of the animosity he held toward Sean Richardson. At the end of the obituary was the announcement of the visitation the next night and the funeral the day after.

"We have to go to this visitation," Rhonda commented after reading the article.

"We as in you and me, or you and Phil?"

"I'm not going in an official capacity. There's nothing to investigate about Mike's death. I feel as though I know his parents after talking to them at the hospital and you were his coach. It's our duty to be there."

~ * ~

The next evening Rhonda and Mark arrived about an hour after the beginning of the visitation. The line was long and from the end of it, Rhonda could see the strain on Anita Yankton's face.

From the obituary, she knew Mike had an older brother and sister. A young man who resembled Mike closely stood next to his mother. Beside him was a woman Rhonda decided must be his wife. The sister stood with her husband and greeted the people who had come to pay their respects. Seated across the front of the room were two sets of older people, Rhonda decided must be Mike's grandparents.

"Mike's older brother Joe played football for us five years ago. He was the captain of the team his senior year. I guess that's one of the reasons Mike was so disappointed when Sean was appointed captain and Mike didn't make it."

Rhonda agreed. Joe Yankton was one of the few players from this area who had made it big in college. Just this past year, a team in the Canadian football league had drafted him. Considering his brother's success, it was no wonder Mike felt slighted when Sean got the position of captain over him.

The line moved slowly, but at last they stood in front of Mike's sister, Ruth Ann. She cried so hard, it was difficult for Rhonda, even with her training, to find the proper words of consolation. It was one thing to confront the family right after an accident happened and quite another to be in a funeral home setting, with the corpse looking as lifelike as possible lying in the casket.

"I didn't know if I'd get to see you tonight, Coach," Joe said, once they moved ahead in the line. "I know all about how Mike and you were getting along at the end, but I don't hold anything against you. Mike's drinking was getting out of control. I saw it for myself when I was back home for Labor Day. We had a long talk about it and he denied everything. I told the folks I was worried, but they told me it was all in my head. I wasn't anticipating it all coming to this, but I wish I could have made a difference for my brother."

"I appreciate your attitude," Mark said. "Mike was a good player. Up until these past few weeks, there never seemed to be a problem."

Joe nodded his agreement, but Rhonda knew there was more the young man wanted to say. Of course, this wasn't the time or the place. She also knew there would be no chance for her to question him further.

"I'm surprised you had the balls to come here," Dan said just low enough for Rhonda and Mark to hear his comment.

"There's no reason why we wouldn't come," Mark said. "Mike was one of my players and an important member of our team. He will be missed. We had a team meeting this afternoon and agreed not only would this season be dedicated to Sean but Mike would also be included. Without them, I doubt we'll do as well as we anticipated, but I know they'll all give their all in memory of their friends."

Anita was the one to answer. "We do appreciate you coming tonight. I understand you have an investigation to do, Rhonda. I've been in contact with Judy Brinks and heard about Mike's involvement in the incident at the funeral home. Even if my husband doesn't come down to talk to you, I will be coming to your office next week. Just let me get past this part of our lives."

"Thank you, Anita. I'll look forward to seeing you again."

They moved on so the many other mourners could talk to the family. "That was interesting," Mark said, once they stood in the reception area of the funeral home.

"To say the very least," Rhonda agreed. "I expected Ruth Ann's reaction as well as that of Dan. It was Joe who really surprised me. It sounds like he saw the problem that Dan and Anita didn't want to address."

"Joe was always a good kid. You know how it is. We can always see things from the outside looking in rather than on a first hand basis. Parents don't want to acknowledge the bad about their kids, especially when the good seems to overshadow everything else. Mike knew how to hide his drinking and still perform not only in school but also on the football field."

"I wonder what made him come to school drunk on Wednesday."

"The only thing I can think is that Dan's attitude toward Native Americans was more than Mike could handle, especially when someone he considered to be one of his closest friends announced his heritage. I think the fact that Sean was captain of the team, combined with me not appointing Mike as captain after Sean's death, pushed Mike over the edge completely."

Chapter Seventeen

With the funeral for Mike Yankton over, Rhonda didn't hear from Adam Brinks until Thursday when she received a call from his lawyer requesting a date for the polygraph testing to be done. Although Rhonda knew what the results would be, the test was set for Saturday morning so Adam wouldn't miss any school.

As she predicted, everything Adam told her had been the truth. With the mystery of the arrangement solved, she realized she was no closer to finding the person who actually fired the shot that took Sean's life than she had been the night of the murder.

"I'm afraid we've hit a dead end on this one," Rhonda commented as she scanned the information in the file on her desk one last time.

"I can't believe you're ready to give up," Phil said. "Usually you're like a bulldog on these cases, even when you aren't the primary."

"Usually I have a list of suspects, but this time everyone I thought could be involved has been completely ruled out."

Before Phil could respond to what she said, her cell phone rang. "Pohs here," she answered.

"Detective Pohs, this is Richard Brave Beaver. I was wondering how you were coming with your investigation."

Rhonda swallowed hard. She didn't like to admit defeat, but in this case she had no choice. "I'm sorry to say we've had no new leads."

"I have had a vision about the boy who died after the car accident. Sean's spirit has come to me and said even though Michael was responsible for the arrangement left at the funeral home for John's visitation, he had nothing to do with Sean's murder. They have been reunited in death and their differences have been resolved. He also said you should look again at the people you have already questioned."

116

Rhonda rolled her eyes. Although she respected Richard's abilities, the thought of going through all the interviews she'd already conducted loomed large in her mind.

"I feel your reluctance," Richard said when she didn't immediately respond. "I can understand your mistrust of this old man, but I assure you it will be worth your time."

"I'm sorry I didn't respond immediately. I just don't know where to start. This has been a very difficult case."

"I know it has, but mark my words, your work will be rewarded with an arrest before the first of the new year. The ancestors have assured me of your success. They are pleased to have you as the one who is investigating this."

They talked for a few more minutes before ending the conversation.

"More conversations with the ancestors?" Phil questioned, waving his hand as though it was all hocus-pocus.

"I know what you're thinking. Richard's visions aren't hocus-pocus. Don't you believe in psychics?"

"Do you? Get real, Rhonda, a lot of that psychic crap is lucky guesses. I realize Richard has been right on about this case, but that was when he was here. I don't see how he can be as accurate being in South Dakota."

"I know it sounds farfetched, but I do trust him. He said to go back over the interviews we've done so far. I know it sounds like a lot of hard work, but what other leads do we have?"

"You're right; we don't have any other options. Where do you want to start?"

Rhonda glanced at the file on her desk. Before they could begin, she received another call. This time it was Anita Yankton on the other end of the line.

"Anita, how are you doing?"

"As well as can be expected. I know I have to come in and talk to you about Mike's participation in that scarecrow business, but something else has come up. I got a call from Crystal Davis. She told me I'm going to be a grandmother."

The number of condoms Rhonda and Phil found in Mike's car flashed in her mind. It was always possible those things could fail, but for some reason she doubted Anita would be a grandmother any time soon, at least not with a child from Mike. "Is this something you're happy about?"

"I don't know how I feel. I would love to have a child of Michael's to love, but I'm concerned about Crystal's announcement. I'm not proud of the fact, but I did know Michael was sexually active. My husband made sure Mike had the best condoms money could buy. I wasn't with my son, but I do know he used protection. He had his heart set on following in Joe's footsteps. You know, playing college ball and then turning pro."

"Accidents do happen, Anita. I hope you plan to have Crystal's baby tested once it's born."

"You bet I do. It's hard enough losing Michael the way we did. I'm sorry to say I knew about his drinking, but didn't do anything about it until it was too late. As far as I'm concerned, Crystal thinks we're an easy mark. It's no secret we're well off."

"Did she ask you for money?"

"She told me Michael knew all about the baby and had agreed to pay for her maternity bills."

"What did you tell her?"

"I said I'd have to talk to my husband, but if necessary we'd do the right thing. She said she needed a thousand dollars in cash immediately. I maintained I wouldn't give her any money, but if she had the clinic contact us, we'd make arrangements with them directly. I certainly don't want to give her cash for anything."

"You did the right thing. I'll check out Crystal's story. Just remember, don't give her or anyone else any cash."

Rhonda ended the call and sat contemplating what she'd just learned. "Well, that was interesting."

"Now what's going on?" Phil inquired.

Rhonda related the conversation to her partner. "I think we need to investigate Crystal's condition for ourselves."

"I take it you don't think she's knocked up."

"I honestly don't know what to think. The first thing I want to do is talk to our IT department. For some reason, I have a feeling Mike isn't the first person Crystal has accused of getting her pregnant."

The IT department provided Rhonda with the print outs from Sean's electronic devices. The stack of paperwork was daunting. When the guys from IT went through it before, they were looking for direct threats to Sean, but nothing else. Now Rhonda and Phil needed to go through each of the messages for themselves.

"How far back do you want to go with these things?" Phil asked.

"Would you believe me if I said back to last spring before Sean went to South Dakota?"

Phil groaned, but tackled the messages from Sean's iPad. "I can't believe the language these kids use," he finally said. "Listen to this one from Mike. *I'm fucking your girl while you're off playing Indian.*"

Rhonda turned to face her partner. "Are you saying you never dropped the F bomb? These kids can't seem to have a conversation without using it. I can remember my folks using that word without giving it a thought. If I don't miss my guess, they have a steady diet of it at home."

"You've got me there, but I never put it in writing."

Rhonda laughed at his response and continued to scan the text messages from Sean's phone. As she did, she found the language equally offensive to that on the iPad, but didn't say anything. Most of the messages on the phone from Mike and Adam all had the same theme. They all taunted Sean about his girl and how he shouldn't be captain of the football team when Mike was more deserving.

"I've got one from Crystal," Rhonda said triumphantly. "It's dated in June, right after Sean left. Here's what it says. *I can't believe you left me here all alone for the whole summer. What if I find out I'm pregnant with your kid? Will you decide to stay out there in the middle of nowhere and abandon me?*"

"Is there any response from Sean?"

"There sure is. *If I thought you were pregnant, you know I'd step up to the plate. Considering we haven't made love without protection, I doubt if you're going to be having my baby.* Her response is, *Maybe I'll*

119

find a new boyfriend, one who will be a father to my baby."

"It sounds like this chick is obsessed with getting pregnant. Somehow she didn't come across that way when we interrogated her."

Rhonda shook her head. "I actually feel sorry for her."

"What do you mean by that? She seems to have it all. Her grades are good, she's a cheerleader and..."

"And she's looking for attention. You can't tell me the attention she gets from her father is entirely positive. As for her mother, I know Sheila and she's a little on the mousy side, to say nothing of being a heavy drinker. That leaves Crystal reaching out for whatever attention she can get. She's the type of girl who can't imagine life without a guy attached to her arm. What's the one way to assure guys will stick around? In case you don't remember, girls like Crystal think it's sex."

"Are you saying she puts out and when the guy dumps her, she threatens pregnancy?"

"That's exactly what I'm saying. I knew a girl exactly like her when I was in school. Mandy Miller was our putout queen. She had the whole package, just like Crystal: brains, beauty and Daddy's money. She made it with anyone she could. Unfortunately, when she got pregnant, she didn't know who the father was. Just because she didn't want to be without a boyfriend, her folks ended up testing over fifty guys."

"Whatever happened to her?"

"The last I heard, she married the father of her baby and then got caught cruising for guys at the plant while her husband worked the night shift. Just last year I found out she'd gone through her fourth divorce and was working on hubby number five. No matter what, she usually comes out of things smelling like a rose. It will be the same with Crystal. I can't imagine that kind of lifestyle, but then I always was a dull girl."

"I just thought of something," Phil said when he stopped laughing. "Remember that e-mail on John's computer. Did we ever find out who sent it?"

Rhonda thought for a moment. "If IT has something, it hasn't come to us yet. Why don't you check on it while I contact Crystal's parents and make arrangements for her to come back in?"

Phil went back to his office while Rhonda placed a call to the

Davis residence. "Crystal, this is Detective Pohs," she said as soon as the teenager answered. "I need to talk to you again."

"Me? I don't know why. There's nothing else I can tell you."

"We just have a few more questions. We'd like your parents to come in with you."

"What are you telling my little girl?" Vern demanded when he came on the line.

"We have some new information," Rhonda replied. "We're going to be doing second interviews with a lot of people. Do you think you can come in tomorrow afternoon?"

"My daughter has cheerleading practice so it will have to be after four."

Rhonda smiled at the apprehension sounding in Vern's voice. "After four will work out just fine. I'll plan to see you then."

Rhonda got to her feet and stretched. It was but a short walk to Phil's cubicle. From the look on his face, she knew the information he obtained from IT wasn't good. "I take it they didn't find anything we can use."

"Not really. The message was sent from a computer at the Madison Public Library and they used a free e-mail address. The information the e-mail people had was bogus."

"Let's put this to bed for the day. It's quitting time. Maybe we'll learn more tomorrow night from Crystal." Phil agreed and put away the files he'd been working on.

"I'll see you in the morning, Rhonda."

~ * ~

Rhonda smiled to see Mark had stopped by her favorite Chinese restaurant for carry out. "You must have had a rough day," she greeted him.

"Rough isn't a strong enough word. With two star players gone, everyone has to give over one hundred percent to make things work. Some of the guys are actually saying this year's team is cursed."

"It does seem that way, doesn't it?" She knew her question

needed no answer. She felt cursed with this one as well. The phone conversations she'd had this afternoon weighed heavily on her shoulders, but she knew she couldn't say anything about any of them to Mark. He was too closely involved in this case, having been the coach for both of the boys who now rested in one of the city's cemeteries.

"How was your day?" Mark asked, as though reading her troubled thoughts.

"It was interesting, to say the very least. You know I can't talk about the case, so let's just enjoy our dinner."

Mark pulled her into a loving embrace. No matter what happened, he knew the way to make everything seem so much better than it had only moments earlier.

Chapter Eighteen

Rhonda spent a restless night. As much as she hoped Mark would say something about any rumors regarding Crystal's alleged pregnancy, she knew she couldn't come right out and ask him. If he volunteered the information, it would be an entirely different matter.

Phil waited for her when she arrived at work. By the look on his face, she knew he'd come up with something on the case. "You look like the cat that swallowed the canary. Did you pull a rabbit out of your hat and mysteriously solve this case?"

"Nothing that dramatic, but I did think of something we might have overlooked. Does it seem strange to you that someone would steal a car in Clinton to drive half way across the county to commit a murder that was, more than likely, planned?"

Rhonda's mind spun. On the night of the murder, they'd focused on Ted and Angie Jacobs. At the time, they'd dismissed the incident as just a stolen vehicle and an unrelated drive-by shooting. With everything they'd learned in the past few weeks, Rhonda knew they were going to have to reinvestigate not only the students at the high school, but also someone in the Clinton area with a motive for murder.

"To be truthful, we've been running in so many different directions, I hadn't given that aspect a second thought. What are you thinking here?"

"Has Mark's team ever played against Clinton?"

Rhonda tried to remember the schedule for Mark's team. She knew Clinton wasn't in the same conference, but that didn't mean anything. As she recalled, there had been a spring baseball tournament for all the schools in the county.

"They don't play football against each other, but if my memory is correct, Sean was an all-around athlete. In addition to football, he played basketball and baseball, Last spring, there was an all-county tournament. It was a charity thing to raise money for the victims of that tornado over by Milwaukee. That was six months ago. I don't see how it could be a factor in our case. I mean, why wait for six months if there was any kind of altercation?"

"I know I'm grasping at straws here, but my gut tells me there's some kind of a connection. Maybe it's something to do with athletics, but I think we need to give it some thought."

"It's something to look into, that's for sure, but we still have to finish going through the messages from Sean's electronic devices. It's possible we could find something, but it means going back even further. I know I'm back to June first, how about you?"

"The message I read from Mike was sent around the Fourth of July. As much as I dislike reading this crap, I know it's something we have to do."

Rhonda sat at her desk and again began the tedious task of reading the numerous messages sent almost 24/7 by today's teenagers. At least it kept them off the phone, but maybe that wasn't so bad. At least the parents of the past knew what their kids were talking about. They weren't texting in a language no adult could ever begin to understand.

Unable to concentrate, she let her mind drift back to the county tournament six months earlier. As she recalled, the event had lasted for two days over the Memorial Day weekend. It had been well attended and each team played their best game. Altogether there had been nine varsity teams and the same number of junior varsity teams.

Rather than continue with the messages she knew needed to be scanned, she accessed her home computer to look at the pictures she'd taken at the competition. Mark labeled the file, MEMORIAL DAY TOURNAMENT, so she had no problem in finding the file she wanted to look at.

It was easy to identify the kids Mark coached not only in football but also in baseball. Sean already sported a dark tan from being at practice all spring. He and Mike looked like best buddies. In the background, she noticed Crystal hanging all over a young man wearing a Clinton uniform.

"Phil, come over and take a look at this picture," Rhonda called across the cubicle wall.

"I thought you were reading text messages."

"I was, but you got me thinking about the tournament. I knew we had a whole folder of pictures from that day. I found this one of Sean and Mike. Do you think the IT department can enhance the background?"

"It's worth a try. I can recognize Crystal, but who's the guy with her? They seem to be pretty cozy."

"That's what I thought. I'll get IT on this and then I'm going to call Nancy Richardson. I need to get a better timeline on the Sean and Crystal relationship."

With the folder of pictures sent to IT, Rhonda placed a call to Nancy. She knew it would come out of the blue and possibly be upsetting, but she had to get the timing of the last few months firm in her mind.

On a legal pad, she put in a start date of Memorial Day weekend. Her project now was to find out when Sean and Crystal broke off their relationship.

"Rhonda, it's so good to hear from you. I was afraid you wouldn't call again after Grandfather's last vision. I'm getting used to it, but at times he's a bit overwhelming. Even Grandmother says he takes a lot of getting used to."

"On the contrary, what he said yesterday got us to thinking. I'm trying to make a timeline for the last few months of Sean's life. I know he was going steady with Crystal. How long did they go together?"

"Let's see, she was his date for the Christmas formal. I was thrilled. She was the first girl he'd ever gone out with and since his father passed away, he just didn't seem interested. Considering she was a neighbor, they'd known each other for years. I wasn't thrilled with Vern calling me all the time to see what the kids were doing. He's very controlling when it comes to Crystal. They dated until school was out in June. I think he had a hard time leaving her behind, but he wanted to spend time with Grandma and Grandpa and I couldn't tell him no. He left on June fifteenth and from what I learned from Vern, Crystal started dating Mike right away. Of course, by then everyone knew about our heritage and Vern made it clear he was glad his daughter had gotten away from Sean. It hurt my feelings, but Sean seemed to take it in his stride. I think they actually went out on a date after he got home in September, but nothing happened with it. He said the only thing she could talk about was how good Mike was in bed. After one date, he told me he'd rather study hard and prepare to return to South Dakota next summer than have to try to compete with someone he once considered his best friend."

Rhonda jotted notes furiously. If Sean and Crystal were going steady in May, why was she so cozy with one of the Clinton players at the tournament?

Her next call was to Anita. "I'm sorry to bother you, Anita, but I have some questions I'd like to ask about Mike and Crystal's relationship."

"You know I'm willing to help you any way I can. What do you need to know?"

"When did Mike and Crystal start going steady?"

"Let's see. I keep a diary. Let me get it."

Rhonda waited while Anita looked for the diary.

"I've found it. Here it is. June sixteenth, Michael said he was going to a party. When he came home, he told me he spent the entire evening with Crystal. That must have been when they decided to get together. I remember telling him I thought she was Sean's girl, but he assured me there was no problem since Sean was off playing Indian for the summer."

"Did they start dating right away after that first night?"

"Oh yes. Crystal came to our Fourth of July party. We have one every year. That was the night Mike asked her to go steady. I remember Dan telling me how proud he was of Michael to have such a beautiful girl for his girlfriend. I think it was right after that when Dan bought Michael the condoms. I didn't want any part of it, but Dan told me I was being a prude. He said all the kids did it and he didn't want any unwanted pregnancy to wreck Michael's future."

"Were they still dating when Mike was killed?" Rhonda knew the question was redundant since she already knew they were going steady.

"Of course they were. I—I've been meaning to call over to the Davis house and ask for Mike's class ring back. I don't feel as though she has any right to it, especially after her call to us yesterday."

"Oh, yes, what did Dan have to say about it?"

"He was livid. He said he spent way too much money to ensure Crystal didn't get pregnant. He wants to fight it and swears he won't spend a penny on Crystal's baby until we're sure Michael was actually the father."

With both phone calls finished, Rhonda filled in the timeline on her chart. Crystal and Sean had dated from December until the fifteenth of June. She'd snagged Mike on the sixteenth of June and started going steady on the Fourth of July. Nancy told her about the one date Sean and Crystal went on in September. It all led to one thing. Crystal didn't like being without a man in her life and the allure of being homecoming queen had more than likely prompted her September meeting with Sean.

"It's time for lunch," Phil said, breaking Rhonda's concentration. "What do you say we stop down at IT and see if they have any of the pictures enhanced for us on our way out to get something to eat?"

"Lunch? Already? Where did the morning go?"

"It seems to me you were on the phone for the majority of it. I, on the other hand, went through more messages from Sean's devices. Did you get anything we can use?"

Rhonda got up to put on her coat. As an afterthought, she grabbed the legal pad with her makeshift timeline outlined on it. "I learned a few things. We can go over them at lunch."

They were both disappointed when the pictures weren't ready, but with the promise of getting them as soon as they got back from lunch, they headed out. Since they could get a secluded booth at Alfresco, they stopped there, knowing no one would be around to overhear any of their conversation.

"The messages I went through were a waste of time," Phil said once their order was taken. "The crap these kids talk about is ridiculous."

"I couldn't agree more, but I don't think it can hold a candle to their sex drive. From what I gathered, Sean was exclusive with Crystal from Christmas to the time he left for South Dakota. I don't know if I can say the same for Crystal. She started seeing Mike the day after Sean left and it only took them two weeks to be going steady. On the other side of the coin, I don't know about Mike, but Crystal went out with Sean in September."

"Do you think they went to bed together?"

"Of course I do. From what Nancy said, Crystal told Sean he couldn't compare to Mike in bed. I think it upset Nancy, but she was glad Sean seemed so focused on what he wanted to do with his life."

Their food was served, ending their discussion. "It sounds like you had Crystal pegged right," Phil said after tasting his soup. "It's hard to believe someone so young could jump from one supposedly serious relationship to another in less than two weeks' time."

"Don't you remember being seventeen? Back then, I bet you were willing to jump the bones of every girl in school."

Phil's face reddened. "I suppose I did, but I was a guy. I thought girls were a little more selective in their partners. I mean, don't they mourn the loss of a relationship for more than a couple of days?"

"Oh, you have so much to learn before your kids hit their teenage years. Girls are just as excited about experimenting with sex as guys are. I think we should look further into Crystal's background when we talk to her this afternoon. I'm willing to bet anything Sean wasn't her first sexual conquest."

Chapter Nineteen

Rhonda stared at the enlarged and enhanced pictures littering her desk. She'd looked through them several times with Mark, but never once had she stopped to look closely enough to see more than the main subjects of the pictures. To her surprise, Crystal cuddled with at least three different players from the various teams represented at the tournament. Some of the pictures were ones she took herself and never realized what was going on behind the people she was shooting.

"This girl really gets around, doesn't she?" Phil asked as he looked at several of the photos she had already been through. "I've counted five different guys here."

"Five? I only saw three. Which two did I miss?"

Phil shuffled through the photos and laid five of them out on the desk in front of her. "The first one is from Clinton, this guy is from Orfordville, this one from Edgerton, this one is from Beloit, and the final one is from Evansville."

Rhonda studied the entire set carefully. The guys Crystal chose were each as different as day and night. Where Sean was blond and Mike had sandy brown hair, the boys in the pictures had dark brown, black, red and auburn hair. One of them had even shaved his head. If no one knew better, they would have thought each of the young men was the most important person in Crystal's life.

"Well, she's certainly a people person. I can see her going far in this life," Rhonda quipped.

"Oh, she'll go far all right. From the look on each of these guys' faces I'm sure they thought she'd end up in their bed before the afternoon was over."

Rhonda's desk phone rang. When she answered it, she was told Vern and Crystal Davis waited for her them in the conference room.

"Well, here we go. I'm almost afraid to start this interview. Vern can be a bit intimidating and I'm afraid he won't allow us to question Crystal about her so-called pregnancy. I'd feel a lot better if when we got there, Sheila was with them."

Rhonda smiled when she saw Crystal sitting between her parents. Although Rhonda knew Sheila was only thirty-five years old, she appeared to be much older. *The booze, that's what makes her appear much older, that and being married to Vern these past years. That man must be a bear to live with.*

"I want to thank you so very much for coming down today," Rhonda began. "I'm especially pleased to have you with us, Sheila."

"I told her she didn't have to come, but she insisted," Vern said, exasperation sounding in his voice.

"Maybe it's time I took a more active role in my daughter's life," Sheila countered. "Just what is it you want to talk to us about, Detective Pohs?"

Rhonda didn't miss the fact Sheila was sober. "There's no easy way to say this," Rhonda began. "Are you pregnant, Crystal?"

A look of sheer terror crossed Crystal's face. "Pregnant?"

"How dare you ask my daughter a question like that?" Vern shouted. "Is this why you dragged us down here? Do you enjoy browbeating children? Don't you know what a terrible time Crystal has been going through? In the past few weeks, she's lost two young men who were very important in her life. We're getting out of here."

"Calm down, Mr. Davis," Phil commented. "Of anyone in this town, Rhonda and I know exactly what's been going on. It's not often we have the murder of a teenager followed closely by the death of another teen in a horrific accident. It's unfortunate that Crystal dated both of these young men, but for that reason we do need to talk to her."

"I'll ask you again," Rhonda said, "are you pregnant?"

Tears ran down Crystal's cheeks but she made no move to answer.

"Answer Detective Pohs, Crystal. Are you pregnant?" Sheila demanded.

"Stop it, Sheila. We all know Crystal isn't pregnant. You're a fine one to talk. Just because you were the biggest slut in high school doesn't mean that Crystal is like you. She's a good girl. She's not out to saddle some poor sap with a kid like you did me."

"Stuff it, Vern. As I recall, you were the one who was hot to trot. You told me I couldn't get pregnant the first time. Well, you were wrong and you've made me pay for it for the rest of our married lives. This is our daughter we're talking about. I'm not going to let you degrade her like this."

Sheila turned her attention directly toward her daughter. "Honey, if you're pregnant, we can deal with this. It's not the end of the world. I was just your age when I got pregnant with you and it was the best thing that could have happened to me. I wish I'd been courageous enough to have raised you on my own. If I had, things might have been a lot different. Now, are you pregnant?"

Crystal nodded. "I've—I've been trying to get the money to have an abortion, but I didn't want to ask you or Daddy."

"Who is the father?" Vern questioned. "So help me God, if I get my hands on the little bastard who did this to you, I'll kill him."

"I—I don't know. I wanted it to belong to Sean, but he wouldn't do it without protection. He said he didn't want to spoil his future."

"You did this on purpose?" Vern shouted.

"Ah—yes—no, I don't know. It just happened. I wanted it to be Sean's baby, but—but he wouldn't make love to me without the condom."

"Then does the baby belong to Mike?" Sheila asked.

"I—I don't know. I met a lot of guys over the summer and it could have been any of them. I've been kinda sorta dating all of them ever since."

"Why did you ask Mike's mother for money?" Rhonda asked.

Crystal looked up, shocked to realize someone other than herself and Anita knew of the phone call asking for money. "I thought if she'd give me the money, I could go to Madison and have an abortion. Then I wouldn't have to think about any of this. When I told Mike I was pregnant, he told me it couldn't be his and he wasn't going to wreck his life just because I got knocked up. I didn't know what else to do."

Sheila put her arm around Crystal's shoulders and allowed her daughter to cry her heart out. "We'll have no more talk about abortions. You'll have this baby and you'll hold your head up high. You're not the first girl to be in trouble and left alone with a baby. Maybe it's best if you aren't attached to the father."

"Bullshit," Vern declared. "I don't care if the father of this child is dead, his family is going to have to pay. I'm not going to raise some dead guy's brat without help from the family."

"Mrs. Yankton said they'd help, but not until they're sure the baby belongs to Mike."

"Crystal," Rhonda said. "I want you to listen to me. I need the names of the other boys who might be the father of your child. For some reason, I don't think it belongs to Mike, do you?"

"Not really. He always used a condom. I didn't like it when he did, because I had sex with some of the other guys without one and it was much better."

Rhonda shook her head. If she lived to be a hundred, she would never understand why young girls wanted to grow up so fast. Of course, with Crystal's family life, it was possible she thought she could do better on her own than with her parents.

~ * ~

Rhonda looked at the names of the boys Crystal had written on the sheet of paper they gave her. There were five names but she had no idea where any of them lived or if any of them could be the father of her child. It was possible the name of the father wouldn't be known until the child was born.

She thought about what had transpired in the conference room. By the time the Davis family left, Sheila promised her daughter she would get treatment for her alcohol addiction. Vern vowed he was going to move out and leave Sheila and Crystal to handle the situation on their own.

Rhonda made a note to keep an eye on Crystal and her baby in the future. She prayed the baby's father would be found and either he or his family would be supportive. "That was quite a session," Phil said once he entered Rhonda's cubicle. "Do you think Vern will leave Sheila and Crystal on their own?"

"It wouldn't surprise me, but I think Sheila will be all right. I do know she's held a job in spite of her drinking. With Vern gone, I have a feeling she won't need the alcohol as much as she has in the past. Just from the little I've learned about that family, I have a feeling he's degraded her ever since they got married. It's entirely possible Crystal and her brother, Chad, have had to raise themselves. If Sheila gets the help she needs, she could easily turn her life around and be a much better parent and grandparent in the future."

As much as Rhonda wanted to start looking for the young men who Crystal had named, she knew it was time to call it a night. Tomorrow would be another day and she knew she'd have her work cut out for her.

Chapter Twenty

Although Rhonda and Phil could identify the schools for which the five young men in the photos played, the numbers on their jerseys were a different story. In most of the pictures, the boys were so entangled with Crystal, even their faces were blurred. It was also unknown whether they played for the varsity or junior varsity teams for their school. Adding to the confusion was the fact there were seven names on Crystal's list, not five. That meant two of the boys were not in the pictures and might not have even been playing for one of the teams.

The first name on the list was Edwin Hardy. After doing a search on the Internet, Rhonda found he was a junior at Evansville and played on the junior varsity team last spring.

While Phil contacted the boy's parents, Rhonda moved on to the next name on the list. Calvin Ashton graduated from Beloit Memorial last June and was in his first year at Blackhawk Technical College.

Bo Parks was a senior at Edgerton. Norman Justice also went to Edgerton but he'd already graduated. He was in the Army stationed at Fort Leonard Wood.

James Alterman was a senior at Orfordville and Herman Hannewell dropped out of Clinton high school and was attending an alternative school in Janesville.

The last one to be found was Blake Swenson from Clinton. He'd also graduated in the spring and was working for his father's tree service.

"How are you doing setting up interviews?" Rhonda asked when she walked the last information over to Phil's cubicle. "Edwin and his parents are coming in after school today. Calvin says he doesn't have class tomorrow morning, so he'll be here by nine. I talked to Bo's parents and they made an appointment for tomorrow afternoon. I still haven't reached James. I did put a call into Fort Leonard Wood for Norman, but

I don't know if I'll hear anything back. That just leaves Herman and he wasn't in school today. I also can't find a home or cell phone number for him."

"At least Blake shouldn't be too hard to find. With this storm, I would imagine both he and his father are hunkered down. There's not a lot of tree work that can be done in this weather."

By the time Edwin came in for his appointment, Blake had been scheduled for ten the next morning. Rhonda certainly didn't look forward to talking to more teenagers, but in this case it was a necessity.

"Just why are we here, Detective?" Edwin's father, Randy asked, addressing his question to Phil.

Rhonda ignored the obvious snub. "I'm sure you know we've been investigating Sean Richardson's death in the drive-by shooting in October."

"You can't think Edwin was involved in that, can you?"

"We're tracking down any lead we can get. One of the people who was close to Sean is Crystal Davis."

At the mention of Crystal's name the color drained from Edwin's face. "We—we only dated a couple of times. She told me her boyfriend dumped her, I felt sorry for her and..."

"Did you have a sexual relationship with Crystal?" Phil asked.

Rhonda could feel the tension in the room begin to mount. No parent wanted to hear their seventeen-year-old son was sexually active.

"Well, did you?" Judy Hardy asked when Edwin didn't say anything more.

"It was only twice. I told her I didn't have any condoms, but she said it didn't matter because she was on the pill. Is there a problem with that?"

"Other than the fear of getting a sexually transmitted disease, nothing really. No matter who you're with you should always take precautions, if for no other reason than for your own safety. In this case, you don't have to worry about anything like that, " Rhonda said in the hopes of calming Edwin down. "When was the last time you were with her?"

Edwin thought for a moment. "We got together right after the tournament in May. We really didn't hit it off all that well. I didn't see her again until just before school started. She called my cell and said she wanted to see me. We drove out to Whitewater Lake and made love on one of the bluffs. I haven't heard from her since."

"Crystal is pregnant," Rhonda said, pausing to see the reaction of Edwin and his parents. "Would you be willing to take a DNA test?"

"Do you think we're going to be grandparents?" Judy questioned.

"We don't know. There are a total of nine young men who have been sexually involved with Crystal. Until her child is born, there is no way to determine the identity of the father. As you know, it's a simple test and can be done at any time and the results kept on file."

"Are you saying Edwin could be branded a sexual predator? I've heard of that happening."

"I doubt there will be any charges. If anyone is guilty of something like that, it's Crystal. The sheer number of partners she's had is proof of that."

"I can't be the father of her child. I just can't be. I'm still in high school. I'm going to college. I'm..."

"We know you have plans for the future," Phil said. "We won't know the outcome of this for several months, but even if you are, things will work out. For now you have to concentrate on your education and think before you act in the future."

"I just have a couple more questions for you, Edwin," Rhonda continued, trying to keep her voice calm so as not to unnecessarily upset the teenager. "Did Crystal ever mention the name of the boyfriend who dumped her?"

"All she said was that he was a jerk. He was going to be gone all summer and she wouldn't have any fun at all. I felt kind of sorry for her. She's such a pretty girl; I couldn't imagine anyone dumping her. Besides, I was thrilled she wanted to be with me. I'd never been with an older woman before."

Rhonda smiled. There was only a year difference in Edwin and Crystal's ages but at that age a year between a younger guy and the girl he's wooing must seem like a lot.

"I think that's all the questions we have for now," Rhonda

concluded. "If we need any more information, we'll be in contact with you. Of course, we'd appreciate it if you would get that DNA test done and the results sent to us. We'll keep you informed as to the results of the DNA test on Crystal's baby."

The members of the Hardy family shook hands with Rhonda and Phil before leaving. "You had that poor kid scared half out of his wits," Phil said. "Do you think he had anything to do with Sean's murder?"

Rhonda shook her head. "I highly doubt it. He's more worried about AIDS and becoming a father at seventeen. I'm sure his folks will see to it that he has protection should something like this happen in the future. I know if I were his folks, I'd be willing to do anything I could to keep him from getting an STD."

~ * ~

Rhonda was surprised when Calvin Ashton arrived at her office. He was a nice looking, well dressed, black man. Being eighteen, Calvin didn't bring his parents with him to the interview the next morning. "I'm of age," he told them once they started asking him questions about Crystal. "I have no problem in manning up. Crystal was a sweet little thing and making love was her idea. I was the one who insisted on using a condom."

"Would you have any problem in having a DNA test?" Phil asked.

"Hell no. I'd be happy to prove I'm not the father of her child. She wanted to do it without protection, but I figured I wasn't the only one making it with her. If that was the case, I didn't want to take a chance on getting something from her. Sometimes you can just tell by looking at a girl how easy she is."

"Did she mention a boyfriend?"

"She said she was seeing someone, but she was planning to call it off. She wanted to be free for the summer."

Rhonda glanced over at Phil. "Would it shock you if we said she'd been dating Sean Richardson?"

"The dude who got killed on Halloween weekend? No way. I'd

be shocked to see her out with him. I knew him through sports and he was so squeaky clean it wasn't even funny. I really liked the guy. It's a shame he got mixed up with her. Of course, he doesn't have to worry about her anymore."

"How well did you know Sean?"

"We met on the football field, the basketball court and the baseball diamond. He was always courteous and didn't make racial slurs like a lot of the lily-white players did. Beloit has a lot of black athletes and we're not always well received by the kids from the primarily white schools. To be truthful, I was shocked when I heard it was a drive-by shooting that took his life. If it had been me or one of my teammates, it would have been more believable."

They thanked Calvin for coming in and compared notes before Blake was due to arrive. "What did you think of Calvin?" Phil asked.

"I think he's one of the most together young men I've talked to in a long time. He certainly has a good head on his shoulders and knows where he's going. I think we've hit a dead end with him."

Before they could compare any more of their notes, Blake arrived. Rhonda was surprised to see his dad with him. With this case, she'd taken no chances. Anyone who wanted a parent present was allowed to have them there. Even at the age of eighteen, they were neither mature nor hardened to the ways of the world and if they wanted the comfort of a supporting parent, so be it.

"I want to thank you both for coming," Rhonda said, as they started the interview.

"Blake has nothing to hide," Frank Swenson said. "It's just the two of us and I know just about everything my son does. What is this all about?"

Rhonda and Phil went through all the questions they'd asked Edwin and Calvin earlier, getting the same answers as they previously heard. Crystal came on to Blake and he'd fallen for her charms.

"Blake and I talked about this and..."

"And nothing, Dad. I can speak for myself. I admit I went out with Crystal, but we didn't go to bed together. I knew she'd been dating Sean Richardson and I didn't want to invade his territory."

"We appreciate your honesty, Blake. We're at a dead end with this case. Like you said, you didn't have a sexual relationship with Crystal, but did she ever talk to you about Sean?"

"I think you're talking to the wrong guy here. Have you contacted Herman Hannewell yet? That guy has been bragging all over town what a good lay Crystal is. He even told me he'd gotten her pregnant, but there were so many other guys, no one would ever be able to pin it on him. The last time I talked to him, he was talking about boosting a car in Clinton and totaling it somewhere outside of Beloit."

The information about the stolen car being involved in the drive-by shooting was something they'd purposely not released to the press. The only information that was released about the Jacobs' car was that it had been stolen and later found totaled. There was no other information put out about it.

"We haven't been able to contact Herman," Phil confided. "We were told he's going to the alternative school in Janesville, but he wasn't in class."

"Alternative school, now that's a joke. He got kicked out of school last year for selling weed. His old man insisted he had to get his diploma but he didn't want him to get a GED, so he enrolled him in that new alternative school. If he's been there a total of three weeks since classes started, it's a miracle. He spends most of his time going to that gentlemen's club out on the highway."

"How can he get in there?" Rhonda asked.

Blake laughed. "I thought you cops were smarter than this. He's had a fake ID for the last two years. He looks older than he is and can get in just about everywhere."

"You've got to have money to do things like that," Phil observed. "Does his father give it to him?"

"I told you, he got caught selling weed at the high school last year. He's doing more than that now. The last I heard, he was going down to Chicago about once a week and selling coke and meth. Since he's already eighteen, the school doesn't report back to his old man."

"Do you have a way to get in touch with him?"

"I do but I can't guarantee he's still using that phone. He buys the disposable ones. He's called me from about six different numbers over the summer."

Blake pulled out his cell phone and read off the number Herman used to place the latest phone call to him. "Like I said, it might be different now. He buys those disposable phones that can't be traced. I don't even know if he can receive calls on this one. I don't even try to call him. He's just not worth the trouble."

"But he keeps calling you," Phil reminded him. "Why is that?"

"We've been friends since kindergarten. When he started getting into drugs, I pulled away. Whenever he gets high, he calls me and wants me to come out and party with him. One time I drove him home, but I decided I didn't want any part of his shit."

"If we go out that way, how will we know if he's there?"

"He won't be there today. This is his day to make his Chicago run. If he goes there at all, it will be tonight, but more than likely he'll be there tomorrow after lunch time. You'll see his truck. It isn't hard to miss. He drives a beat up red nineteen seventy-eight Dodge Ram. He's got the thing decked out with more lights than the landing field on an aircraft carrier. There's a lot of rust on it, but somehow he keeps it running."

With the interview ended, Rhonda thanked Blake and his father for coming in to talk to them. Armed with the new information, she was glad they only had one more interview today and tomorrow they could plan on staking out the gentlemen's club. Hopefully their surveillance would be productive.

Bo Parks' interview followed along the same lines as all the ones they'd conducted earlier. He'd met Crystal at the tournament and they'd dated consistently throughout the summer. They hadn't had sex until late August. At that time, he'd used a condom, but was more than happy to have a DNA test. When asked about Sean, Bo knew who he was but Crystal hadn't mentioned the fact they'd been dating. He was even surprised to find out about her involvement with Mike Yankton.

"I'm exhausted," Rhonda said as they decided to wrap up their day. "At least we got more information than we had before we started."

"I'm with you on that one. I did have a call back from Fort

Leonard Wood. It seems Norman's about to be deployed to Iraq. They assured me he was there on the night Sean was killed and they would send us the information on his DNA, but it's unlikely he's the father. He's been at basic training since the end of July. Considering Crystal wasn't showing yet, I have a feeling she didn't get pregnant until the end of August or the beginning of September. That rules him out entirely for instant fatherhood."

Rhonda agreed. It sounded as if Norman Justice was in the clear. At least the military had been cooperative and they'd been able to rule out yet another suspect in this case.

Chapter Twenty-one

"You know that stakeout you were planning for today?" Sheriff Cantwell greeted Rhonda and Phil when they came into work the following morning. "You don't have to go out to the gentlemen's club this afternoon."

"What are you getting at?" Rhonda asked.

"Herman Hannewell was in a traffic accident last night just over the state line on I-ninety. When the paramedics cut him out of his truck, they found cocaine with a street value of over a million dollars. He's in police custody at Beloit hospital.

"How badly is he injured?" Phil finally asked.

"He won't be walking out of the hospital any time soon, if that's what you're getting at. He's still unconscious, but he has a bad spinal cord injury. It's possible he'll spend the rest of his life in a wheelchair."

Rhonda took a deep breath. Even though she knew Herman faced a sentence of life in prison, she wondered which would be the worst punishment, the prison sentence or the one of being trapped in the chair.

"Has he been read his rights?"

"Not yet. We thought you might want to do the honors. I want the two of you to get down to Beloit and be the first ones to question him."

Rhonda looked at Phil in disbelief. What they thought was going to be a day filled with a boring stakeout had suddenly turned into being able to question their main suspect in the Richardson murder.

At the hospital, they showed their badges and were allowed access to Herman's room. Rhonda wasn't quite prepared for the pimply-faced young man in the bed with his hand shackled to the side rail.

"It's about fuckin' time someone came in to see me. Why the hell am I handcuffed to this fuckin' bed?"

Rhonda approached the bed and looked Herman directly in the eye. "You're here because you were in an accident and you're handcuffed because you were transporting cocaine across state lines." Before she continued, she read Herman his Miranda rights.

"Why the hell do I need those?"

"Because the lady just arrested you."

"You're sure making a hell of a big deal out of some dope. Everyone fuckin' does it, man. If they legalized it, we wouldn't have all this drama."

"Herman Hannewell, you're under arrest for possession of a controlled substance, car theft, and murder," Rhonda said.

"Murder? Who the fuck got murdered? I sure as hell didn't fuckin' murder anyone."

"I'd suggest you watch your language, young man," Phil warned. "You have been implicated in the theft of a vehicle registered to Ted Jacobs of Clinton. Not only are you implicated in stealing it, but it was also wrecked. The stolen vehicle was seen leaving the scene of a drive-by shooting on Halloween weekend."

"Look man, that shooting wasn't my idea. I just wanted to go for a little joy ride. Who knew I'd end up wrecking the bitch?"

Rhonda pulled a chair up to the side of the bed. "If the shooting wasn't your idea, why did you participate?"

"I wanted a piece of ass and the chick said I'd get it if I did the driving. She's one hell of a good fuck. We've been getting it on all summer but after she went back to school, she said we had to cool it. I had a snoot full of coke and well, you know about those urges."

"Does this chick have a name?"

"Sure she does, it's Diamond or Emerald, or some kind of stone. I just know her number when I want to get laid."

"Is it possible her name is Crystal Davis?"

"Yeah, that's it, Crystal. I knew it was some kind of a stone."

"So what did she have to do with the shooting?"

"I don't know if I should say anything more. I mean, you got me dead to rights on the coke, and I don't sweat charges for taking that dude's van, but I don't want no part of charges for murder. I want that lawyer you said I could have."

Reluctantly, Rhonda backed off. Once a suspect evoked his right to counsel, she knew there was no use in pursuing any further questioning.

"So what happens to me now?" Herman asked. "You said if I couldn't afford an attorney, I'd get one. Do I get one of them public defenders?"

"I doubt it," Phil said, sarcasm dripping from his words. "With the amount of money you've been making selling drugs, I'm certain you have enough money stashed somewhere to pay for a lawyer, and a good one. We'll call your father and have him retain one for you."

"That's a fuckin' laugh. My old man ain't gonna call a lawyer for me. He hates my guts, except when I come home with enough coke so he can get high. Maybe that Crystal chick can get me a lawyer."

"I doubt it. She has enough problems of her own. Is there anyone else you can contact to help you out on this one?"

Herman's demeanor changed dramatically. "It's just me and my old man, but I got an aunt who might call someone for me. I don't got my phone. I don't know her number."

"Give me her name and I'll look it up for you," Rhonda offered, taking the local phone book from the desk drawer.

They waited while Herman placed the call. He just finished talking to his aunt when an unkempt older man entered the room.

"What the hell kind of trouble have you gotten yourself into this time, you worthless whelp," the man demanded.

"Just who are you?" Phil asked confronting the man.

"And for that matter, how did you get in here?"

"Herman here is my son and I waited 'til that cop at the door went to the john before I came in. Why is there a cop at the door and why is he handcuffed to the bed? Ain't that police brutality or something?"

"Your son is under arrest. He's just called someone to retain a lawyer."

"A lawyer, what the hell for? What I heard was he got in a car accident."

Rhonda watched as Phil took Herman's father out to the hallway to advise him of the charges against his son. They had no more than left the room when the bedside phone rang. Since Herman couldn't answer for himself, Rhonda picked up the phone.

"This is Herman Hannewell's room, Detective Rhonda Pohs speaking."

"This is his Aunt Judy. He called me about retaining a lawyer for him. I talked to our attorney and he's on his way to the hospital now. Is there anything else I can do for my nephew?"

Rhonda felt sorry for the woman. From the sound of her voice, it was evident she cared about Herman. "I'll let you talk to him."

She handed the phone to Herman and monitored his conversation with his aunt. With her standing right there, she knew the young man would be guarded in what he said on the phone.

An hour later, the lawyer Herman's aunt retained arrived. "I'd like a moment to confer with my client," he told Rhonda after the initial introductions were made.

Rhonda and Phil stepped out of the room. "Do you think we'll get anything else from him?"

"That depends. I think we ought to talk to the DA. Something tells me he might want a deal. It seems like everyone watches *Law & Order* these days and that's the first thing to come out of their mouths. If it's true he was only the driver, maybe he thinks if he rolls over on the guy who actually pulled the trigger, he'll talk for a lesser charge."

While Rhonda was still contemplating her answer, the door to Herman's room opened and the attorney came out. "My client would like to talk about getting a deal on this one."

Rhonda nodded. "We'll put in a call to the district attorney's office."

~ * ~

By quitting time, Rhonda's mind was reeling from what Herman said in exchange for a lesser charge being filed against him.

According to Herman, Crystal promised he would be part of a threesome if he stole a car and drove to the K-Mart parking lot. When he got there, he saw Crystal and a guy named James Alterman from Orfordville waiting for him.

Crystal explained how she wanted to scare the shit out of the guy who'd dumped her. While Herman drove, Jim rode in the front passenger's seat with Crystal riding in the back and giving directions.

The fact Crystal was involved made Rhonda sick to her stomach. The very thought of arresting a pregnant teenager was distressing.

"I just talked to Sheriff Cantwell," Phil began as they got into the county car to drive back to the station. "He assures me warrants will be issued in the morning for the arrests of both Crystal and James. For tonight, we're done." He flipped shut his cell phone and took his seat on the passenger's side allowing Rhonda to drive.

She drove back to the station deep in thought that this had been a nerve wracking case, the likes of which she hoped she'd never have to contend with again during her career.

Chapter Twenty-two

While Phil executed the arrest warrant for James Alterman, Rhonda made an early morning visit to the Davis home. From the cars parked in the driveway, she knew she and the uniformed officer arrived prior to the family leaving for work and school.

A marked squad car driven by another female officer and another by her male counterpart, pulled into the driveway behind the SUV and sedan parked in front of the double garage door, followed Rhonda's unmarked car. Her heart pounded and her stomach churned as she got out of the car and went up to the front door. Making arrests always excited her, but this one was different. This time it was a kid.

Standing on the front porch, she pushed the doorbell. Hearing it ring inside prompted the excited barking of a small dog. It wasn't that she didn't like dogs, but they always complicated the situation.

The door opened and Rhonda came face to face with a very stern looking Vern Davis. "What the hell are you doing here?" he questioned.

"We have a warrant for Crystal's arrest for the murder of Sean Richardson."

The little dachshund continued to bark and nip at Rhonda's ankles. Instinctively, she reached down to let the little dog sniff her hand. As she expected, after a few seconds the barking stopped and the little brown dog began licking her hand. From the expression on Vern's face, she knew he considered the dog a traitor.

"This is an outrage," Vern spat as the female officer handcuffed Crystal and read her the mandatory Miranda rights. "I thought we told you everything you wanted to know the last time we were in your office. Isn't it enough that my daughter is pregnant and we're not certain who fathered the little bastard? Why can't you leave us alone?"

"We've learned more information in this case and it does

implicate Crystal. We are taking her down to the station to have her booked and then taken for further questioning."

"I want to go with her," Sheila said between sobs.

"I'm sorry, but Crystal is eighteen. It's not mandatory for a parent to be present for questioning."

"If that's not a crock of shit, I've never heard one," Vern declared. "Now listen to me, you little bitch, don't say a word until I get there with a lawyer to represent you. Just keep your mouth shut, do you understand me?"

Crystal stood mute, tears running down her cheeks. Rather than answer her father, she nodded her head in understanding.

"I just can't believe you think Crystal had anything to do with Sean's murder," Sheila sobbed. "She's never been in any trouble before."

"If that's not a crock of shit," Vern said, as he reached out and slapped Sheila right in front of Rhonda. "That little bitch has been nothing but trouble since the day she was born. After this pregnancy fiasco, I don't put anything past her."

By the time Vern finished his tirade, Rhonda had stepped between the couple. "I'm placing you under arrest for domestic battery, Mr. Davis," Rhonda said, pulling his hands behind his back so she could cuff him.

"You can't be charging him for that," Sheila shouted.

"It is and I am. I saw him strike you. That is domestic battery. It happened easily enough that I believe it's something you're used to. You don't have to continue living like this. If you want to press charges of your own, you're free to do so."

After reading Vern his rights, he started to leave Sheila standing alone and shocked in her kitchen.

"Call our lawyer," Vern called over his shoulder. "Tell him to get his ass down to the sheriff's department. If he doesn't, there'll be hell to pay. Do you understand me, Sheila, hell to pay!"

The male officer escorted Vern from the house until finally his ranting was no longer audible in Sheila's neat kitchen.

"Are you all right?" Rhonda asked, knowing the answer to her question. Blood trickled from a small cut at the corner of Sheila's mouth and a bruise on her cheek was already evident.

"I will be. It's not the first time he's hit me. My dad always hit my mom. I just thought that's the way things were supposed to be. It's one of the reasons I drink."

"It's not right for a man to put his hands on you for any reason. Does he hit the kids?"

From another room, she heard someone call for Sheila. Rhonda turned to see a boy of about fourteen enter the room, pushing himself in a wheelchair. "What's going on, Mom?" he asked.

Sheila quickly told her son what was going on, then made the introduction of her son Chad to Rhonda.

Chad held out his hand and gave Rhonda a firm handshake. As he did, he looked into Rhonda's eyes as though reading her mind. "I was in a car accident. It's not as bad as it looks. I'm not completely paralyzed, but things are much easier in the chair."

"I have to go down to the sheriff's office," Sheila said. "Will you be all right here alone?"

"You know I will, Mom," He turned his attention back to Rhonda. "I do home schooling. It's a lot easier than trying to maneuver the halls with my chair. Besides, Dad says I'll embarrass my sister. In case you haven't noticed, she's the star of this family. Dad just tolerated Mom and me. It's okay, we have each other and for now that's enough."

Chad took a long minute to study his mom's face. "He hit you again, didn't he? I wish I could get out of this chair and defend you when he goes off like that. It's not right, Detective Pohs. I know it's not right, but Mom keeps saying that's what her dad did to her mom. It sucks."

"Well, a lot of things might be changing, Chad. I just arrested your father for domestic abuse. Even if your mother doesn't want to press charges, I witnessed it and I'll be charging him."

"Do it, Mom," Chad pleaded. "We can get along without him. I know the only reason you drink is because of the way he hits you without warning. I want to go down to the sheriff's office with you."

"What about your schoolwork?" Rhonda asked.

"The program we use for the home schooling has the lectures taped. I can access the one I was going to listen to this morning anytime during the semester. I won't get too far behind. As a matter of fact, I'm at least two weeks ahead of my class. Missing a day or two won't hurt me too much."

"If you want to be there, you can go," Sheila assured her son. "We'll be out there right after Chad has his breakfast."

Rhonda nodded. "It will take us that long to get both Crystal and Vern processed and into the system."

"Are you sure Crystal is guilty of this?" Sheila inquired.

"I'm afraid we are. We have a confession from one of the other young men who was involved. We are also arresting another young man this morning in connection with this case."

Sheila shook her head sadly. "We should have never given her so much freedom. Vern said she needed to find herself. When she was going steady with Sean, Vern was very upset. He said she should be meeting more people. Well, it looks like she met people, but what kind of people did she meet? How could someone with so much going for them end up like this?"

~ * ~

When Rhonda left the Davis home, a second squad had come to take Vern into custody. Assured Sheila would arrive at the Sheriff's Department shortly, Rhonda drove the short distance in deep thought. Her mind went back to her first interview with Crystal. At the time, she had completely dismissed her as a suspect in Sean's death. With the information that had come to light in the past few days, she was forced to rethink her position.

The scene that greeted her at central booking was like something out of the reality TV show *American Jail*. Crystal sat with the other women who were being booked for everything from prostitution to shoplifting, while James and Vern sat with the men.

"Are you the son of a bitch who said my daughter was involved in that drive-by shooting?" Vern shouted "If I get my hands on you, I'll wring your scrawny neck."

"You got it all wrong. I didn't roll on the bitch. She must have rolled on me. All I wanted was a piece of ass and when she offered me a threesome, I wasn't going to refuse her. Whoever taught her how to give a guy a blowjob and take a butt fucking did a damn good job. She's hot as a pistol and one of the best I've ever had."

Rhonda exchanged a surprised glance with Phil. She was grateful the surveillance cameras caught not only the image but also the audio of the exchange between Vern and James.

"Do you think we'll get any of them to actually confess to the murder?" Rhonda asked.

"If I'd had a tape recorder going in the car, I'd have our confession. As soon as I identified myself, James knew why I was at his door. As for his father, he's a real piece of work. I got to their place at seven this morning and the old man had a beer in his hand. He told me it was about time someone came to take away his piece of shit son. As for James, he was more concerned about who turned him in than anything else. I'm sure he thinks it was Crystal who gave us his name and told us what he did."

"Do you think he was the shooter?"

"There's no doubt in my mind about that. I called in for a search warrant and there should be some uniformed officers out there now looking through that place. You won't believe what it looked like out there. No one should be living in those conditions. I'm pretty sure I saw a rifle. That's one thing I asked to have brought in. I'm sure ballistics will prove it's the gun that killed Sean."

Rhonda studied James. As much as she wanted to see a clean-cut teenager, the boy who sat across the room looked as though he was in need of a good bath and a haircut.

"Where you got my kid?" an obviously drunk man shouted as he came into the booking area. "That son of a bitch took my kid away and then let those cops into my house. They ain't got no right to go through my things like that."

"Your son is under arrest, Mr. Alterman," Rhonda said. "I would suggest you get him a lawyer."

"Oh, now I get it. We can't afford no lawyer, so we get picked on. It's always the poor who are the scapegoats for anything the fuckin' cops can't solve. I suppose you're one of them lesbian women who like to throw their weight around, but I want to talk to a real cop."

"I'd watch my mouth if I were you," Rhonda said, her blood starting to boil.

"Shut your fuckin' mouth, bitch. I want to talk to a real cop and I want to talk to them now."

"Well, you're talking to me. I'm the lead detective on this case. Now, as we told your son, if you can't afford a lawyer, the courts will appoint one. Those are your options."

"Listen to her, Dad," James called out. "I've already asked for a court appointed lawyer, so why don't you just shut up?"

Rhonda breathed a sigh of relief. This unkempt young man spoke intelligently and put his alcoholic father in his place. Rather than wait to see what else would transpire between father and son, Rhonda went into the interrogation room and prepared for either Crystal or James to come in with their lawyer to answer the questions she and Phil had to ask.

Within a half an hour, Crystal Davis, Sheila Davis, and Crystal's lawyer were in the interrogation room. Since Crystal was seventeen, it was only natural for her mother to be with her in addition to her lawyer.

"Crystal and I have been talking," Sheila said, initiating the conversation. "We've decided it's best for everyone involved if she just tells you the truth. Our lawyer agrees with us entirely."

"What do you want to say, Crystal?" Rhonda asked.

"When Sean came home, I wanted him back in my life, but he'd moved in a different direction from me. I dated a lot of guys over the summer and I was afraid I was pregnant. I thought if I could get Sean to sleep with me without protection he'd think the baby was his and marry me. I know my dad married my mom when she got pregnant with me. Of all the guys I dated, I wanted Sean to be the man to be a dad to my child. He didn't want to do it without protection and that made me so mad. He was just like Mike, he didn't want to be a father to anyone."

"What did you do about it?"

"I remembered that Sean's grandpa always dressed up like a scarecrow for Halloween. I thought if I got Herman to steal a car and have Jimmy shoot over his head I could go to Sean after it was all over and tell him I was there for him. I didn't know he was taking his grandpa's place. I also didn't know that Jimmy would kill anyone. When I found out it was Sean, I was devastated. I knew he would never marry me and I'd have to work harder on Mike to get him to get me pregnant."

"But you knew Mike wasn't the father, right?" Phil asked.

"Of course I did. He used those expensive condoms and bragged about how much his dad paid so he could have all the fun he wanted."

"So how did you get Herman and Jimmy to go along with your plan?" Rhonda asked.

"I knew they both liked dirty sex. I told them I'd do both of them at the same time if they did what I wanted."

"Did you have sex with both of them?" Sheila asked, as though completely shocked by her daughter's confession."

"No. We were all freaked out and then Herman wrecked the van. There was no way I wanted anything to do with either of them again. I saw that pumpkin head explode and realized Jimmy killed Sean's grandpa. Everything went so terribly wrong. I just wanted to go home and pretend none of it ever happened. The next morning I heard it was Sean who had taken his grandfather's place. I just wanted to die, but I knew I had to live for my baby. I didn't think anyone would accuse me of doing anything. I just wanted to have my baby and live happily ever after. I thought for sure Mike would marry me and then he got killed. Everything has gone so wrong."

Chapter Twenty-three

Rhonda felt completely drained after questioning both Crystal and James. In light of not only Crystal's confession but also Herman's, James' lawyer insisted he should confess as well.

"What's going to happen to Crystal now?" Sheila asked when she met Rhonda in the hallway.

"That's not up to me. Any charges will come from the district attorney's office. There are several charges pending, including car theft, leaving the scene of an accident and murder. Whether or not she wanted anyone hurt, Sean lost his life. Someone has to be held accountable."

"What about Crystal's baby? Will the courts take it away?"

"Not if someone takes responsibility for it. Is it possible you and your husband will be willing to raise it while she's in prison?"

"I will be responsible for it, but without my husband. What you witnessed this morning wasn't anything new to me. When you arrested him, I realized it was time for me to grow a backbone and stand up for myself. Once this business with Crystal is settled, I'm going to file for divorce. Chad and I deserve a better life than the one we've been living. I can't save my daughter from prison, but I can make certain my son and my grandchild are well cared for. I have a good job and will be able to support us."

As soon as they stepped into the reception area of the sheriff's department, they were met by members of not only the press but also the local radio and television stations. Rhonda was relieved when Sheriff Cantwell gave the mandatory interview with the press. In it he gave Rhonda the credit for solving Sean's murder as well as the theft of the Jacobs' vehicle.

Before leaving the office, she placed a call to Mark. "What's up, honey?" he greeted her.

"I thought you should know we made three arrests in Sean's murder case today. One of the boys was from Clinton and he's the one who stole the car. One was from Orfordville and he was the shooter."

"Do I really want to know who the third one is?"

"I'm afraid you do. It was Crystal Davis. She wanted to scare Sean's grandfather and then comfort Sean in the hopes of having him marry her and give her baby a father."

"She's—she's pregnant?"

"I'm afraid so, but we won't know who the father is until after the baby is born. During the time she got pregnant she was 'with' at least seven guys other than Mike. I'm afraid there will be more horrors coming to light before this is all over. We also arrested Vern Davis for domestic abuse and Sheila is pressing charges."

"What a bombshell. Something tells me you knew most of this last night. It's no wonder you didn't get much sleep. Let's go out and have dinner tonight, so we can both relax and digest all of this."

~ * ~

By Christmas, Rhonda's prediction of more horrors coming to light had come true. Sheila Davis filed for a divorce after kicking Vern out of their house.

Through Crystal's lawyer, they learned Vern had been sexually abusing his daughter for years. It was no wonder she craved the sexual attention of the many guys she dated.

She had been taught, at an early age, to please men. Unfortunately, her obsession with Sean ended up costing him his life.

After the arrests became public knowledge, Rhonda received a call from Richard Brave Beaver. He told her how proud she'd made him and invited her to come to South Dakota the next summer for a vacation and to learn more about the way of life of the Sioux, the way Sean would have lived his life if it hadn't been cut short.

Although she knew the New Year would bring three trials in which she would be involved, she decided to enjoy Christmas with her husband and look forward to the coming year.

Also by the Author
at
Rogue Phoenix Press

Man in the Lake
Rhonda Pohs Mysteries Book Three

Rhonda Pohs has been hired as a token woman on a small town police force. Other than traffic stops on the highway, her only other duties are to meet with families after a loved one has been killed in a traffic accident. A call from a distraught wife about her missing husband comes in just before one of a man floating in a local lake. Chief Franks send Rhonda to check on one of the most cheating husbands in town. While Rhonda is talking to Kitty Reedman, she is informed that the man floating in the lake is Karl Reedman, Kitty's husband. From the get go, Rhonda is embroiled in solving the mystery of Karl's murder at the risk of her life.

Murder in the Meadow
Rhonda Pohs Mysteries Book Three

As Rhonda moves to a detective position with the county sheriff's office her first lead case is the murder of the most hated man in the county. George Atkins has been killed with his own pitchfork while spreading manure. The fact the elderly man was out in a raging blizzard makes no sense. Why would he be out in such inclement weather? As the case progresses, threats are made against other members in the family, until Rhonda finally reveals the most unexpected suspect with a deep seeded hatred for the Atkins family for what he believes has been done to him in the past.

About the Author

Sherry Derr-Wille began her writing career in her sophomore English class in high school. Challenged to get an A on the first test, she won the right to sit in the back of the room and write for a year. At the end of the year no one told her to stop the assignment, so she didn't. At her 40th class reunion, she realized she was the only one who enjoyed the assignment. It was too late because by that time she'd signed seventeen contracts for her work.

Wife to her high school sweetheart of over fifty years, she is the mother of three, grandmother of nine and great-grandmother of seven. She is retired and lives in a mid-sized town close to the Illinois border in Southern Wisconsin. Her mantra is READ LOCAL AND BE TRANSPORTED TO ANOTHER WORLD.

VISIT OUR WEBSITE
FOR THE FULL INVENTORY
OF QUALITY BOOKS:

http://www.roguephoenixpress.com

Rogue Phoenix Press
Representing Excellence in Publishing

Quality trade paperbacks and downloads
in multiple formats,
in genres ranging from historical to contemporary
romance, mystery and science fiction.
Visit the website then bookmark it.

www.ingramcontent.com/pod-product-compliance
Lightning Source LLC
Chambersburg PA
CBHW050742230626
47052CB00004BA/1042